Puffin Books

Galax-Arena

'All the suffering and pain of their lives were cancelled out
by the beauty and courage of the performers. I understood
for a moment why they put their entire being into the
performance, even though they were being used like slaves
and animals. In the Galax-Arena they were free.'

Confronting and stunningly original, *Galax-Arena* challenges
our way of thinking about the world.

Galax-Arena *was named an Honour Book in the 1993
Children's Book Council of Australia Children's Book of the Year
Awards. It was also shortlisted for the 1993 Victorian Premier's
Literary Award (children's books), the 1993 TDK
Australia Audio Book Award and the 1994 South Australian
Festival Awards for Literature.*

'Innovative, provocative, effortlessly ethical and utterly
convincing . . . a brilliant book'

Katharine England, *Advertiser* (Adelaide)

Also by Gillian Rubinstein
Space Demons
Answers to Brut
Melanie and the Night Animals
Beyond the Labyrinth
Skymaze
Flashback
At Ardilla
Foxspell

Picture books

Squawk and Screech
Dog In, Cat Out
Keep Me Company
Mr Plunkett's Pool
The Giant's Tooth
Peanut the Ponyrat
Shinkei
Witch Music
Annie's Brother's Suit

Compiled by Gillian Rubinstein

After Dark
Before Dawn

GALAX-ARENA

Gillian Rubinstein

Puffin Books

Puffin Books
Penguin Books Australia Ltd
487 Maroondah HIghway, PO Box 257
Ringwood, Victoria 3134, Australia
Penguin Books Ltd
Harmondsworth, Middlesex, England
Viking Penguin, A Division of Penguin Books USA Inc.
375 Hudson Street, New York, New York 10014, USA
Penguin Books Canada Limited
10 Alcorn Avenue, Toronto, Ontario, Canada M4V 3B2
Penguin Books (N.Z.) Ltd
Cnr Rosedale and Airborne Roads, Albany, Auckland, New Zealand

First published by Hyland House Publishing, 1992
This Puffin edition first published 1994
10 9 8 7 6
Copyright © Gillian Rubinstein, 1992

Offset from the Hyland House edition
Made and printed in Australia by Australian Print Group, Maryborough, Victoria

National Library of Australia
Cataloguing-in-Publication data:

Rubinstein, Gillian, 1942–
Galax-Arena
ISBN 0 14 036100 6.
I. Title.
A823.3

for Jane

Acknowledgements

The author, in writing this book, was assisted by a
Category A Fellowship from the Literary Arts Board of the
Australia Council, the Federal Government's arts funding
and advisory body.

Australia Council
for the Arts

Thanks to George Turner for his advice on
contact languages.

Glossary

amigo	friend	muddah	mother
cabeza	head	nada	nothing
chillun	children	niño	child, son
ciudad	city	noch	night
cyan	can't	obeah	
dar	door	woman	wise woman
desaparecida	disappeared one	pass	happen
		peb	the people of the Galax-Arena
dess	death		
di	day		
Earss	Earth	sab	know
espiritu	spirit	saft	soft, gentle
familia	family	segreto	secret
flar	floor	sho	so
ganja	marijuana	spik	speak, talk, say
ken	can		
ketch	catch	triste	sad
lak	like	trus	truth
los altos	the heights, high place	tyam	time
		wan	one
manyan	morning	wyatt	white
milagro	miracle		

We've been in this town two months. That's quite a record for us. Our father keeps us on the move. He thinks it's safer. We don't go out much, don't mix with other people. We hardly even talk to each other. We're supposed to forget what happened, but it seems that if we can't talk about that one thing, we don't feel like talking about anything else. So we exist in silence.

We are me, Joella, now pretending to be called Sue, my brother, first called Peter, now known as John, and my sister (Liane/Sally).

There are only the three of us here. We don't know what happened to the others. Our father thinks they were probably deported, but he says it's too dangerous for us to try and trace them.

I know it's stupid but every time there's a news item on television about refugee camps I strain my eyes peering at the faces, hoping to see Mariam or Fenja, and whenever there's news of street kids in South America, I think one of them might be Eduardo, or even Leeward.

We watch a lot of television. In all the rented places and motel rooms we've lived in that's the one thing that always stays the same. Last night Liane and I were watching a gymnastics competition, and I saw Allyman.

Peter – I've decided to use our real names in this story,

because I'm trying to tell the truth – wasn't watching. He never watches this sort of thing. I guess it reminds him too much of what he used to be and what he is now. One of the worst things about being on the move is that you never have any private place of your own, and Peter feels this badly. So whenever we arrive somewhere new he claims one piece of furniture as his, and no one else can sit on it. Last night while we were watching television, he was sitting out the back in an ancient green armchair, practising writing with his left hand. He refuses to go to school since he turned fifteen. He says his writing is so bad there's no point.

I saw Allyman clearly, in the crowd, the pale face and the long red hair unmistakable. Liane said nothing about it. I don't know if she saw him or not, but she had a terrible nightmare later and in the end none of us slept much.

So today while I was sitting dizzy with tiredness and anxiety in a school I don't even know the name of, among kids who have no idea how lucky they are, the idea came to me that I might as well write the whole story down. Because no matter how we try and forget, it really happened and it's still going on. No one's going to try and stop it. No one's going to do anything about it. We couldn't do anything to stop the others disappearing. We couldn't do anything about getting an inquiry going. We ended up being totally helpless, hiding in isolated towns, always terrified someone's going to catch up with us. I can't stand the idea of spending the rest of my life like this. The only thing I've ever been any good at is seeing the truth, so the only thing left for me to do is try and write it down. And when I've got it written down, I'm going to go back to Aunt Jill's to live, and I don't care if they come and find me there or not.

It's right that I should end up the story teller because, in the old days, I was always the one who was the audience. I spent the first thirteen years of my life on the fringe of Peter's story, watching it unfold dazzlingly, watching my unusual, gifted brother excel, without trying, in everything he did. And as if that wasn't enough to keep me on the sidelines, since I was seven there was Liane coming up from behind with her newsreel face and her orphan history and her special place in my mother's heart.

But that was before the time we spent in the Galax-Arena. That was when we were still ... I was going to say *an ordinary Australian family* except that we never were an ordinary family. We always seemed to be different from everyone else. Our father, Hayden, was too old and too clever to be a typical dad, and our mother was too young and too crazy to act like an average mother. For a few years they made an effort to be ordinary. They provided us with a house in an outer suburb where we went to the local school, Peter won prizes in Little Athletics, Liane got distinctions in ballet exams and I had lots of pets, but all this came to an end when Sylvie, our mother, decided it was stifling her and she needed what she called time out. We were supposed to stay on in the house with Hayden, but he went very strange after she left. He took us out of school on bush camping trips and tried to teach us survival skills. He made Peter do the driving even though he was way too young to get his licence and he drove so recklessly that Liane and I were always terrified of crashing.

Hayden had lots of ideas but he wasn't very practical so we were always getting stranded, running out of food and water and having to find waterholes and eat bush tucker. Apart from being allowed to drive, Peter hated it. He and Hayden spent the whole time arguing. Peter actually ran away a couple of times. He said he hitched rides back to the city and lived on the streets performing and busking, but he was always back at the house, or staying at a friend's place when we got home so I never knew whether to believe him or not.

That was our life before. Before we knew Leeward, Allyman, Mariam and all the others. Before we were kidnapped ...

It started for us, as for most of the others, with a journey. People on journeys are easy to make disappear. Accidents are arranged, buses never arrive, children vanish on the road from here to there.

Our journey began at Central Station, being put on a train going north. Our last camping trip with Hayden had ended up with Liane in hospital for two days with serious dehydration and we were being sent to Casino to stay with our aunt, Jill, his older sister. She lived on her own on a small property and kept a couple of house cows, some chooks and an old mare. Our grandmother (Sylvie's mother – she was actually younger than Jill, and only a few years older than our father) came to make sure we got on the train. She'd had to take a day off work to come up from Cronulla and she was angry. Her anger was mostly with our parents, but we got the effects of it, not them.

Peter was furious with them too, and he took it out on Nana, Liane and me. Liane was miserable. She adored Peter and when he was unkind to her she retreated inside herself. She wouldn't talk to any of us. She just held her special toy, a glove puppet rabbit called Bro, up close to her face, and bit its fur. Bro was a weird toy. It had been Peter's and he gave it to Liane when Sylvie first brought her home. To begin with she was terrified by it. She had a lot of nightmares and tantrums and she would scream at the rabbit, throw it against the wall and stamp on it. But when the nightmares lessened, she started carrying it around everywhere with her, talking to it endlessly, and pretending it answered her.

I was angry and miserable too, fed up with our parents for making such a mess of our lives, grieving for our animals that we'd had to find other homes for since Hayden would never remember to feed them – but I was excited about the journey too. I couldn't wait to get out of the city and I was glad we were going to Aunt Jill's.

Aunt Jill liked me. Without boasting, I could say I was almost the only person she liked. It was a family joke that she hated everybody. So it really meant something that she liked me, and she didn't like Peter.

Not that she'd ever said so. I just knew. I'd always known things like that. Peter used to call me the Witch because I'd tell him something and it'd turn out to be true. I had no idea how I did it. Perhaps I've got an extra eye that picks up on the things most people don't notice. I used to spend a lot of time lying next to Tam, our cat, and Jake, our terrier, and trying to feel life like they felt it. Once I spent the whole afternoon lying on the grass next to Jake and all of a sudden I started noticing how many different things I could smell and for a flash of a second I thought I was a dog. Dogs and cats are very sensitive to people's moods and they always know who likes them and who doesn't. Perhaps I learned to do the same thing from Jake and Tam.

Most people, even Hayden at the height of an argument, looked at Peter and smiled. At that time he was a sort of golden person, in looks with his copper coloured hair and brown skin, as well as in everything else. Golden people are fine to have around, but sometimes it's hard being their sister.

Aunt Jill didn't seem to notice that Peter was a golden person. She wasn't the least bit interested in how people looked or what they could do. She judged everyone by if animals liked them or not, and if they could get up cheerfully at five in the morning, one of the few things I could do and Peter couldn't. She grumbled at Peter for spooking the cows and for not getting out of bed till halfway through the day. She didn't grumble at me. She gave me little pats on the arm, as if I was one of her animals, and she always bought Crunchy Nuts, which were my favourite cereal, and not Coco Pops, which were Peter's.

Of course as soon as I started to realise some of what had happened to us I realised it was Peter that *they* were after. It was Peter that drew *their* attention to all of us. Perhaps *they* wanted Liane too. She was very good at dancing and gym even then, and striking looking, but Peter was the star. When I thought I recognised Hythe at Casino station, it was probably because I had caught sight of him somewhere before, watching Peter, following him, just as

I had glimpsed Allyman at the gymnastics competition. Hythe didn't want to take me. From the start he discounted me. I was always going to be disposable. He just thought it would be easier to take me than to leave me on my own . . .

But here memory brings me up short with a jolt. We are standing on the platform at Casino station. It's cold – it's six o'clock in the morning and the sun is not yet over the land, though it's light and we can hear magpies. We're all a bit spaced out – we've been sitting up all night, dozing in between stations and waking to look at the dark bush flying past, and we're even more fazed by the fact that Aunt Jill is not here to meet us. Instead this stranger in moleskins, old Drizabone and brown Akubra is telling us that our aunt's car has broken down, and one of the cows is calving early, and she's asked him to come and pick us up.

It sounds so plausible; he even knows our names. He uses them casually as if he has known us all our lives and the fact that he obviously knows us makes us think we know him. Also, I am sure I've seen him before.

We're shivering with cold and it seems to make sense to get into the man's Landcruiser – it looks just like the sort of thing a neighbour would have, but as I'm following Peter across the station forecourt it suddenly feels wrong. I'm sleepy and my thoughts won't put themselves together properly but I've picked up on something that's signalling urgently to me. I stop and look at the man, who is walking ahead of me, carrying Liane's bag, and holding her by the hand. He throws the bag into the back of the Landcruiser and lifts her into the cabin. She's still clutching Bro.

'Peter!' I shriek, as my brother is about to climb into the Landcruiser too.

This is what I remember – the man's look. He turns. He sees me. He knows I suspect something. He hustles Peter into the car and gets in himself. He starts the engine.

He is going to leave me behind!

I run to the car. Peter's door is still open.

'Wait,' he's saying. 'Wait for Joey.'

'Peter!' I hiss. 'Get out! Something's wrong. We musn't go with him.'

My brother is embarrassed. He likes the man. He trusts him. And now, his sister (the Witch) is about to go over the top in her crazy way.

'Hop in,' he says, trying to sound calm and grown up.

'She doesn't have to come,' the man says with an indulgent grin. 'Jill could get over later after the vet's been and she's got the car fixed. You just sit down there and wait, honey.'

I read him clearly. He doesn't want me to come. Well, stuff you, I think and I climb into the car next to Peter.

2

The first thing the man said to us when we were in the car was, 'You must be perishing. I brought a flask of coffee. Anyone want a drop before we go?'

We all muttered, 'No. No thanks,' rather shyly. He made us feel shy because he was so attractive. I remember thinking he looked just like someone on television and he talked like someone on television too, with a slight American twang that made me think of heroes.

Now I can't hear that accent without shuddering. Much later I found out it was the same voice that had phoned Aunt Jill before daybreak and spun the lies to her that kept her on the farm so she never came to Casino station to meet us, never gave a second thought as to why our parents had changed their minds again about sending us, except to grumble at their fecklessness and unreliability.

But at the beginning we liked his voice. It was the voice of a trustworthy good guy.

'Well, I'm going to have a drop,' he said, cheerfully, not in the least put out by our refusal. He reached over to the back seat, and as he did so, the sleeve of his coat fell back a little, and I caught sight of a silvery covering, like a heavy bandage, on his right forearm. He brought out a thermos and a plastic box, in which were cups, a little bottle of milk and some sugar, and chocolate biscuits. He poured a cup of coffee for himself.

Perhaps it was the coffee smell, perhaps it was the cosy look of the cups and the bickies – anyway, Peter said suddenly, 'I'll have a cup, after all,' and after that Liane and I both said, 'Me too please.'

The coffee contained the first drug – some kind of upper that made us all feel very happy and confident. We forgot about the long train journey and the fact that we were meant to be staying with our aunt. We forgot the things our parents had told us about how to behave and how to look after ourselves. All their warnings had nothing to do with what was happening now. In fact our parents seemed like the most unreasonable and blind of people, whom we should never consider again. We felt as if we were on a fantastic magic mystery tour. By the time we were beyond the town and heading out through the scrub and paddocks we were all giggling and laughing, and we thought the man driving the car (Hythe, he told us his name was) was the greatest guy in the world.

He told us crazy jokes. He drove at top speed down the dirt roads and across creek beds, making the Landcruiser lurch from side to side so the little shark that hung from his key ring danced madly in the ignition. He gave us chocolate biscuits and more chocolate. He sang and did television ads and comedy shows in all the proper voices. Even Liane, who didn't laugh very often, surrendered completely to him and made little choking giggles in her hands.

My suspicions had gone under, but after a while something began troubling me through the high I was on. We seemed to be travelling for a very long time.

'Peter,' I tried to whisper to him, 'Where are we going?'

'Round and round in circles!' Peter replied, not quietly at all. 'Excellent, hey!'

'This isn't the way to . . .' and then I stopped. With one part of my mind I knew we were meant to be going to Aunt Jill's, but the part of my mind that was uppermost didn't care about this fact in the least. It wanted to go driving on like this for ever, laughing and joking and being happy. I can remember frowning and gritting my teeth as I made a huge effort to speak.

'Aunt Jill's,' I said, stumbling over the words. Then I reached out and tried to tap Hythe on the shoulder. 'This isn't the way to Aunt Jill's!'

'Joella, babycakes!' he turned and grinned at me, his perfect film star teeth flashing white against his deep tan. The Landcruiser bucked and swayed as it hit a rut in the track. The shark swung. 'Don't be scared, babee! Trust me! We're just gonna go have a bit of fun.' Then he began to sing to the tune of *Maria*.

'Joella!
Joella!
I've just met a girl named Joella!
And suddenly I've found How wonderful a sound
Can be!'

And I fell for it. It's one of the things I'm really ashamed of. Just because that dreamy looking guy sang a corny song with my name in it, I started to grin like an idiot and for a couple of moments I felt as happy as I'd ever felt in my life.

The others joined in and we were all warbling away, 'Joella! Joella!' when we rounded one last corner and there smack in front of us was the rocket.

Memory's telling lies here, of course. It wasn't smack in front of us, because people don't actually leave rockets lying casually around in the bush. What was right in front of us were all the trappings of an air base – security fences, guard blocks, a cluster of domed buildings, aircraft and, alongside the buildings, gantries looking just like the ones we'd seen on countless television programmes, the silver cone of the rocket easily visible between them.

We were all silenced by the sight of it, except for Hythe, who went on whistling cheerfully as the Landcruiser headed towards the gates.

They opened for us immediately and Hythe gave a casual wave to whoever was inside, a wave which turned into a thumbs up once we were through. The gates closed electronically behind us.

I didn't like the thumbs up at all. It made me think of Mission Completed, and other military phrases.

Peter didn't like it either. 'Hey,' he said sharply. 'Where is this place? Where are you taking us?'

Hythe didn't answer. He gunned the Landcruiser towards the rocket. There were several men in silver overalls working purposefully around it and when they saw us coming they stood still and waited for us.

Liane was still singing Joella/Maria

'Say it loud and there's music playing!
Say it soft and it's almost like praying!'

Hythe took up the refrain but Peter and I were silent. It was hard to feel afraid through the drug, but beneath the excitement I could feel a sort of cold dread waiting to come surging up from below.

'What is this?' Peter said, outrage starting to show in his voice. 'Stop! Take us back!'

'Don't be scared,' Hythe replied, his voice as jokey and friendly as ever. 'It's all going to be fun fun fun! Just a little ride in a spaceship. Just a little game of space pirates.'

'Peter,' I said, trying not to giggle, because it sounded so ludicrous. 'We're being kidnapped!'

'By space pirates!' he said back, disbelief, laughter and fear all mingled in his voice.

Liane didn't say anything, but she was gazing at the rocket and clutching hard onto Bro, all ideas of singing along with Hythe obviously gone clean out of her head.

And then everything was very confused. I don't remember getting out of the car and into the rocket very clearly. It's like that when people hurry and hustle you. You're trying to cope with the hustling, and their determination, and you don't quite notice what's happening to you.

I remember being carried up the narrow stairway, and inside the flight module. I remember overalls being pulled on and Liane complaining because her hair got caught on the velcro. And then I was pushed into a seat and given something else to drink.

Peter tried to fight them, but it was no good – one smallish fourteen year old boy against seven or eight grown men. They weren't angry about it. They laughed as they restrained him and got him fastened securely in the seat.

'Little tiger, aren't you,' Hythe said admiringly and touched him with a gesture halfway between a punch and a caress. Peter tried to bite him.

Liane's face had gone mask-like with terror. She was holding Bro Rabbit up against her mouth and biting his fur.

That's the last thing I remember clearly. The two bites. As though we were already turning into what they wanted us to be – into animals.

3

The next part I can remember only in fragments.

The noise – the shriek of the engines as the launch began. The terrible pressure that flattened us back into our seats and stretched our faces into unconsciousness. And the nausea that waited for us every time consciousness returned, along with total screaming terror.

I had no idea how long it went on for. When the pressure stopped weightlessness began, even more nauseating and disorienting. My eyes ached so I could hardly see and my tongue was huge and itching with thirst.

The sensation of iced drink in my mouth and the realisation that relief of thirst must be the most wonderful feeling in the world. Hythe's voice, soothing and crooning, explaining what was happening, even though I could hardly hear.

His voice goes on and on, repeating the same phrases over and over.

You're feeling the G force now. The acceleration has to be enormous to get clear of the Earth's gravity. We're travelling at 11.2 ks a second to get out of the gravitational well. Then we accelerate to 13 per cent of the speed of light before we make the leap to hyperspace, once we're clear of the solar system.

Heading for a planet in the Cygni system.

Vexak.
Inhabited by an alien race called Vexa.
To perform in the Galax-Arena.

Images of space pass before my eyes. The blue-green, white-streaked Earth spins and shrinks and disappears. Stars red-shift behind us, darkness cones ahead. Hythe, moving around the module, curses the Coriolis effect as he drifts sideways. And the relentless, haunting words continue to whisper inside my mind, mingled with his treacherous, joking tones. *Kidnapped. Space pirates. Aliens. Vexa. Galax-Arena.*

Finally darkness so complete it seemed like death. Nothingness. Not sleep, not unconsciousness, but something much deeper and darker. And being called back from it – days or years later? – by that same warm, cheerful, friendly voice.

'Joella! Joella! Wake up, honey. Time to get up, babycakes!'

I opened eyes that seemed to have been sealed shut for a million years. Hythe, looking pleased with himself, was bending over me, shaking my shoulder. I sat up sharply, more to escape his touch than anything else, for with the sudden movement darkness threatened to return again. He tried to stroke my hair, but I wriggled away. I wasn't going to let him near me. I felt hatred like I've never known for anyone grip me hard in the pit of my stomach.

'Calma! Calma!' he said, and made a reproachful face at me, but he didn't try to touch me again. He went to wake up Liane. She opened her eyes painfully, sat straight up and spat in his face. I often used to worry about if I really loved Liane or not – it's not as if she was my real sister and when she first came to live with us, when I was seven and she was four, it was pretty hard to get used to having her around. But at that moment I'd have died for her.

'Heyy, kidlings!' Hythe said, wiping his face with a silky-looking pink handkerchief and sounding hurt. 'Whassa matter? You angry with your old pal?'

'What the heck do you think?' Peter said ferociously. He was up, and prowling round the room we'd been sleeping in. He didn't look too bad though his skin was a shade paler than usual, making his copper hair brighter and his emu eyes more piercing. 'Where are we? What is this place? How're we going to get home?' Then he stopped in mid-breath and muttered bitterly. 'Nearly forgot. We don't have a home to go to, do we.'

That brought a moan from Liane. She clutched Bro Rabbit to her face and sobbed desperately into his fur. At that moment I wished I was her, and could sob into a furry toy too. As it was I could feel huge tears starting to form in my eyes and something swelling up in my chest.

'That's fine, honey,' Hythe said gently. 'You cry it out. All of them do that at first. They all cry their eyes out to start with. But they get over it, most of them. And you'll get over it too. You're going to be a big star. You're going to be the greatest.' Then he smiled charmingly and contritely to us, turned to open the door panel, and left the room. The door slid shut behind him.

Who all cry their eyes out to start with? I was wondering. There must be other people here, other children? And what are we here for? What is the Galax-Arena?

I looked around. We were in a small windowless room. There was no way of telling we were millions of miles away from home. Or was there? I frowned as I tried to work out what it was that made the room alien. Its proportions didn't seem quite right, as if it had been designed by M.C. Escher, the artist Hayden likes so much. And there was a very strange smell, not unpleasant, but not earthlike in any way. The room had the chilly artificial feel of air-conditioned places back on Earth ... and yet the air itself felt *different*. I shivered.

Peter called from the only doorway apart from the one Hythe had left through. It led into a tiny bathroom, with a shallow bowl in the floor, a basin, faucet and buttons. Peter pressed one. The water that came out was an extraordinary colour, a sort of fluorescent pink. We both put out a hand at the same time to touch it. And it felt . . . it's hard to describe but it felt slippery.

Our hands flew back from the water and I grabbed Peter's. We stared at the horrible pink water sliding slowly down the drain and we both started to sob at the same moment.

That's how we spent the next few days – though we did not notice that days were passing. Nothing existed but our grief and our loss. Everything we loved was gone for ever, we did not know why, or even how. We had thought our first loss bad enough. When Sylvie had left and Hayden had gone round the twist, I'd thought our grief and anger could never have been greater. Now that state seemed like paradise. Now even the worst days back then, when everything was black seemed beautiful, compared with this alien place. All of us, even Peter, called out for our parents in despair and cried ourselves into a state of stupor and apathy.

Some children never came out of this state. They pined away until they woke no more and slipped into death. So Leeward told us later. And there are two in particular who still haunt my dreams. But one of the things I've learned is that human beings are tough and the urge to live is powerful. Little by little our urge to live returned.

All the time Hythe cared for us, fed us and held drinks to our mouths while we did not care if we lived or died and everything tasted of ashes. I didn't remember our parents ever giving us the loving attention he gave us then. When you are completely alone you come to care for your captor, even if you hate and fear him. I guess this is how zoo animals feel about their keepers. They hate them because they keep them prisoner, but they love them because they bring food and water. That's how I felt about Hythe. We all did. We looked forward to his visits, his jokes and his caresses. Before long we began to talk to him when our meals were brought.

I don't know how many days went by before this happened. The rooms we were in were lit artificially and the lights went off when it was meant to be night time and on again in the morning. Our watches had been taken away, so we had no idea of time. Our body clocks were all out of sync anyway, and the dark nights seemed interminable.

'What's the length of day on this planet, wherever it is?' was one of Peter's first questions. He seemed recovered. I think he just got bored with grieving.

'Vexak is part of a solar system around a G2 star very similar to our own Sun.' Hythe replied patly. 'It revolves on its axis once every seventeen and a half earth hours – but of course the whole time structure among the Vexa is based on their own astronomy which is why it would seem very erratic to you.'

'Why can't we go outside?' Peter's eyes were showing some sign of their old hard gleam.

'You're living within the Galax-Arena – that's my name for it, catchy, huh? It's specially built for Earth people, with simulated Earth atmosphere, gravity, light and so on. The Vexa are humanoid, but they have a different metabolism from us. You wouldn't survive for ten seconds outside. So don't go trying it, right, baby? I'm getting kind of fond of you guys, I'd hate to lose you.'

'Huh!' Peter made a scoffing noise through his nose. 'Whatever chance have we got of getting outside? And if we did get outside what then? We're never going to get back home, are we?'

'Yeah, man, that's the way the cookie crumbles. You can't always get what you waaant, as the song goes!' Hythe grinned at us endearingly. 'You got it in one. You can't go home anymore. That's another song, ain't it?'

We said nothing to him. We looked at each other. We knew it was true and in that moment we accepted it. We didn't exactly forget Hayden and Sylvie, Jake and Tam, Aunt Jill and all the other things that made up our old lives, but we drew a curtain over them. We let go of them. We started again.

'Well, what are we here for?' Peter said slowly.

'That's my boy!' Hythe crowed with delight. 'I knew

you'd come through. I knew you'd make it! Soon as I set eyes on you I said to myself, I said, that kid's a winner. That kid's got what it takes. That kid's going to be a star!'

'A star at what?' Peter said, coolly because he was pleased and didn't want to show it.

'A star in the Galax-Arena, babycakes! In the greatest show in the galaxy.'

I didn't say anything because I was too busy trying to grasp what was going on underneath. Hythe was hard to read because he was always lying. Everything he said was false in one way or another. So it was difficult to tell if everything was totally false or if he was just fabricating extra bits on the surface.

Liane asked, 'What is the Galax-Arena?'

I looked at her and realised that she had recovered too. Thin and delicate though she looked, she was one tough kid. I wondered if having already gone through so much loss and exile made it easier for her to adjust. And then the bleak thought came to me that even here, unbelievably far from home, our family relationships were unchanged. Peter and Liane were still the stars, and in-the-middle Joella was still the one nobody noticed.

Hythe confirmed this by tickling Liane in the ribs and saying as she squirmed away from him, 'That's where you're going to perform, pretty baby! Cos you're going to be a little old star too. Old Uncle Hythe can pick 'em, believe you me.'

You spat at him, I reminded Liane inside my head, but she'd forgotten. That was in the past and all over now. I could tell that she was as hooked by his jokes and his flattery as Peter was. They were both intrigued by him. They wanted to perform and compete. That was what had always made life thrilling for them. But what about me?

'What about me?' I couldn't help saying it out loud.

'You can have a shot too, honey. Why not? That's what I always say.' Hythe's voice dripped with fake concern and sincerity. 'You never can tell. Sometimes a kid'll really surprise you. You go for it, Joey. And if you don't make out, if it doesn't happen for you, one of the Vexa'll most likely take you as a pet. You're a cute kid, even if you ain't no gymnast.'

'What do you mean, a pet?' It was Peter who asked it. I was too busy trying to sort out the relative falsehoods of Hythe's last sentence. The outstanding one was that I was not what people usually called a cute kid, never had been, never would be. And I definitely didn't like the idea of being a cute kid pet to a Vexa.

'Now listen to me,' Hythe said, sounding more and more folksy with every word, 'You kids have been to Marineland, Ocean World, that sort of place, haven't you? You've watched the whales and the dolphins go through their tricks? You've done that, right? Right?'

We nodded silently as the comparison started to make sense to us.

'Waal, youall had a ball, dincha?'

'No!' I interrupted truthfully. I've only been to Marineland once and I hated it. I hated seeing the dolphins doing their tricks with such a wholehearted sense of loving life, while idiot people sat and gaped at them, and ate chips and drank soft drinks and ooed and ahed.

Hythe ignored me. 'Now you're the dolphins, and the Vexa have fun watching you! You learn the tricks and the more difficult they are and the harder you work the more fun the Vexa have. Get it?'

'But we're not . . . animals,' Peter said hotly. 'We're human beings.'

'Not to the Vexa you ain't, baby! As far as they're concerned you're animals, clever, fascinating animals. Not Vexa. Therefore not people.'

'I think you're a criminal,' I said slowly, after a pause while what he had said sank into our overloaded brains.

'What do you get out of it?' Peter demanded indignantly. 'You're . . . you're nothing more than a slave trader!'

'Heyy, hang about,' Hythe replied, hurt. 'I'm a professional! I'm an acrobat and a trainer. I take what I do very seriously. I'm proud of it. I'm proud that I can put on the finest shows in the galaxy. I was a star once myself. Get an eyeful of this.'

He stepped out of the tracksuit he wore, revealing strong, hairy muscular shoulders and a silver singlet like a circus performer's. The silver was the same colour as the bandage that covered his forearm. He sprang lightly forward and stood perfectly balanced on his hands, took one hand away and stood on the other, flipped over into a cartwheel and leaping upwards did a double somersault in the air.

'You're going to teach us to do that sort of thing?' Peter said. I could hear the eagerness in his voice.

'That's just kid's stuff,' Hythe said nonchalantly. 'Sure, I'll teach you that for starters. But you're going to do the real thing. You're going to hit the big time. I'm gonna teach you everything I know, and more. I picked you out. I travelled across space and time for you kids, never forget that! You're going to be the greatest!'

Liane and Peter were hanging on his words. I said, 'But you stole us.'

'Joey,' he said, 'You've got no idea how that suspicious mind of yours hurts your old uncle.'

'And I bet they pay you a lot,' I went on. 'Somebody must be paying you a packet for it.'

'Yeah, yeah,' he replied sarcastically, 'I get Vexa credits straight into my Swiss bank account. How much do you think it costs me to run this place? Not to mention the Skyshark.'

'The Skyshark?' Liane questioned.

'That wonder of technology that gets me around the galaxy. My state-of-the-art spaceship.'

'Would the Skyshark take us home again?' I asked. The word 'shark' made me think of something, but I couldn't remember what.

'What do you want to go home for?' he said persuasively. 'Your planet's stuffed. You belong to a doomed race. I saved you. Look at it like this. You're going to be safe here. What's life on Earth anyway? Nasty, brutish and short as the philosopher said. If the Big Bang doesn't get you then the Greenhouse effect will, and if the Greenhouse effect doesn't, then there's always AIDS. You don't have to worry about that any more. You don't have to worry about anything. You'll never be hungry or cold or unemployed. You're far better off here. Aren't you grateful to your old uncle?'

He made such a funny, pleading face that Liane couldn't help smiling.

'Atta girl!' he said, ignoring the fact that I was still scowling at him. 'That's enough chat now. Too much talking always gives me a headache! You all look pretty fit. Let's get to work!'

4

We took off the clothes we'd been travelling in. They were filthy. I was glad to get out of them. I never saw them again. When we came back from the pink-water shower, Hythe gave us new clothes. Not new, for they showed signs of wear. Other clothes. They were like leotards, in dullish shades of brown material that fitted as close as skin. Mine was too tight, chafing under the arms and between the legs.

When we were dressed Hythe stood back and gave us an appraising look. 'Not bad,' he said, pleased with himself. 'Your old uncle always did know how to pick 'em!' But when he looked me over, he clicked his tongue as though he was thinking of something else. Then he opened the door with a card key, and we stepped out of our tiny prison into a huge circular area. There were many other alcoves like ours, their doors open. My eyes flickered round the place. It had the same emptiness a school has at the end of the day. Many people had been there recently. Where were they all now? Who were they?

In between the doors and over the tops of the arches were shelves, hooks and cubbyholes, filled with decorations and brightly coloured clothes, like costumes for exotic callisthenics. Liane's eyes opened wide and she looked as if she was going to grab the stuff and start adorning herself with it.

'Later, later!' Hythe said with a smile, taking her by the arm and pulling her close to him. 'Won't you be the prettiest little thing ever, hey, babycakes?'

We skirted the mats and low tables in the centre of the room, and crossed to huge double doors at one end. These too slid open, unlocked by another of the card keys. I looked sideways at the bundle in Hythe's hand, trying to count them. There seemed to be fifteen or twenty at least. Ten alcoves, a key for each one, left ten other doors between us and whatever lay beyond.

Freedom? No, the alien landscape and atmosphere of Vexak. There would never be any freedom for us. We were trapped here forever.

The double doors opened straight into an elevator. My feeling of dread increased almost unbearably. The thought of getting in that narrow space, and feeling the floor drop away, made me shake.

Peter stepped straight in. Liane hesitated only to slip Bro Rabbit onto her hand. Hythe let go of her and took my arm. What had been affectionate suddenly became cruel, though he still smiled, still joked.

'Get in, honey,' he coaxed me. 'Ain't gonna bite you.'

He was holding me with his left hand. When I held back, unable to make myself walk into the elevator, he raised his right arm.

I thought he was going to hit me. I flinched back. But it was worse than a blow. From the silvery bandage that covered his hand came a sickening buzzing that penetrated right into my brain. It hit the place where language begins, so words became scrambled and thought impossible. The person that was *me*, that made me *Joella*, began to dissolve.

Hythe dropped his hand. The girl stepped into the elevator. I saw her from a great distance. Her face was ugly with fear, her body clumsy and ill-formed.

The elevator doors closed. Hythe stroked the girl's hair. 'Don't make me do that again, hey, baby? I hate to have to hurt you.'

The girl said nothing. She was trembling. Her skin was prickling. Cold sweat broke out on her forehead and under her arms. I smelled her fear. My own fear. She and I became one again. I didn't want to be her. She had made Hythe angry by disobeying. Hythe didn't want her. I hated her. Ugly girl. Witch.

Liane and Peter, backs to the wall, stared at me as though I was an outcast. Later I myself felt the shared panic when Hythe used his hand on one of us but then I didn't know that they were shaken too. I thought they were turning against me.

To stop tears falling, I looked around the elevator. It had buttons with letters on them and, next to the letters, strange symbols. I didn't have time to count them then, but later I did: there were twenty-one of them. We went from the second lowest level – R – to the one above – G. The lowest level (the button below R) was labeled E & P. Again Hythe had to use the card keys to operate the elevator.

'G stands for ground,' Liane said, as we rose soundlessly.

'Not here, honey,' Hythe replied. 'Here G stands for two things. Gymna and Galax-Arena. And first I'm going to show you the Gymna.'

'What's on all the other floors?' Peter said, touching the buttons.

'Nothing to interest you, pal. And you can't get to any of them, so there's no use you trying, get it?'

'I know that!' Peter responded swiftly, half-smiling. 'So when do we get to see the Galax-Arena?'

'When you're ready for it. Won't be long for you, trust me.' Hythe reached out and gave Peter the same half-punch, half-caress, on the side of the face, that I remembered from the struggle in the rocket. This time, though, Peter didn't try to bite. He grinned, and as we left the elevator he couldn't disguise his pleasure and his eagerness.

I'd seen that eagerness so often before. It was one of the things about my brother that made people smile. I hated him for it. I felt as if it betrayed me.

Hythe strode along, whistling cheerfully to himself. The sound echoed off the metallic walls of the passage, which was actually more like a tunnel or a huge pipe curving round a central circle.

We trotted to catch up with him, following him like dogs. Peter and Liane had recovered from their fear and were acting like dogs too, dogs let off the leash, running up the sides of the tunnel and dropping lightly down almost from the top, bounding along, pushing each other, filled with energy and enthusiasm.

I had never felt less like gambolling in my life. I was still shaking from Hythe's punishment. And I was both terrified, and trying to find something to hang on to that would help me survive. I'd always been the sort of person who liked to feel earthed, to know exactly where I was. I'd always had a very good sense of direction. But here, there was no way I could orient myself. No fixed point anywhere in my world. Nothing to take my bearings from. I didn't know if we were above ground or below – if the planet Vexak had what I would call ground or if it was made up of other totally unknown elements. The only invariable I had was the alcove we had spent so much time in. I knew where that was in relation to where I was now – below, but on the same circle . . .

Peter interrupted my thoughts to say to Hythe, 'We're not floating about, so gravity must be pretty much the same on this planet.'

'This place has simulated gravity,' Hythe said. 'A lot of terraforming has been done. The Vexa are excellent engineers. The whole thing is spinning.' He took Peter's hand and guided it to the walls. 'Feel it?'

We all put our hands to the walls. There was a faint vibration running through the smooth metallic curve and for a moment I felt vertigo, as if we were indeed spinning at an unbelievable speed.

'Wow!' Peter said.

'Why don't we feel as if we're going fast?' Liane said, frowning.

'We're moving at the same speed,' Peter explained. 'It's all relative.'

'Exactly!' Hythe crowed, and for a moment there was a

flash of something on his face which I couldn't quite place. But then I forgot it until much later, for we came to a set of doors giving access to what lay beyond the inner wall of the tunnel. Hythe inserted yet another card, and the doors slid open.

We heard briefly a pounding of feet and shrill shouts. They stopped abruptly as Hythe said, 'Welcome to the Gymna.' We stepped inside into silence.

Despite the colourful clothes we had seen below, there was nothing glamorous about the Gymna. It was a rehearsal area. The kids in it were drab and unglamorous too – *kids* – that's what I called them inside my head until I learned that the words kid or child were as insulting to them as nigger or wog. They called themselves the *peb*.

There were about twenty of them. They hung from every level, like birds in an aviary. They were as thin and delicate as birds, a flock of sparrows or starlings in the dull-coloured leotards that merged with the brown and black skin.

And after that one moment when everyone stared at us motionless, they flew to us like birds, chattering and calling in patwa, a strange broken English that we could hardly understand.

'Ware ya fram? Wat lan ya live fo? Wat dey call ya?'

'Take it easy, take it easy,' Hythe said, fending the pressing peb off. He was not angry, but his right arm was slightly raised, and the peb were as aware of it as animals the whip. They kept one eye on it constantly and, while they sought his attention, they were always poised for flight. He cleared a path through them and pushed us into the centre of the area. 'Give them a bit of space. Plenty of time to find out all that. They ain't gonna run away.'

He said all this in his usual cheerful, friendly way and, though he pretended to cuff them, as often as not the cuff turned into a caress.

'Where's the boss?' he shouted over the giggles and the fluting voices. 'Where's my man? Where's Leeward?'

He did not speak patwa. He only ever used it in contempt or anger. He assumed everyone would understand him whatever he said, and they mostly did. They grasped his meaning from his tone of voice and his body language as much as his words. Later I would realise, because I became like that myself, they knew him better than their own mothers, better than they would ever know anyone, because every gesture of his, every changing mood, could mean life or death.

A girl with thick black hair that fell in a heavy fringe over almond eyes set in an arrogant face, replied, 'He on los altos Hyd. He fo up!' She used the pidgin English mockingly, as though she despised it yet deigned to speak it for the sake of the others. I thought she was beautiful and I wanted her to like me. Her gaze caught mine and she stared me down. I could feel myself flushing.

Two girls with fine, identical features and long, elegant limbs like deer were also staring at me. Their hair was braided into tight complex patterns and their skin was brown and perfectly smooth. One of them put out a hand and touched my face wonderingly, then said something to her twin and laughed.

My face was burning. Among those slender, smooth skinned children I felt solid and lumpy and clumsy. I could also feel a kind of despair building up in me. All the things Hythe had said before, the hints he had dropped and the comments he had made now formed themselves together in a perfectly clear picture. These children were all performers, gymnasts and dancers. Even as they clustered round us they could not stop dancing. They turned themselves upside down and walked on their hands as naturally as on their feet. Every now and then one or other of them would leap into the air and turn a somersault or burst away from the group to go tumbling across the floor. They rippled and quivered with energy.

I'd never felt more disposable. There was no way I could even begin to attempt the things they could do. A forward roll was the extent of my gymnastic ability. I'm just the wrong shape for gym. The wrong shape for most things, I think. All I seem to be able to do is see the truth, but no one wants to listen.

I felt my death sentence had been signed. Terrible tears

started to form in my eyes again – I thought I'd none left to cry but tears never seem to dry up – and to stop them falling in front of these bold, clever acrobats who despised me enough already, I tilted my head and looked up.

The Gymna was high and rose to a domed ceiling from which were suspended battens that held trapezes and ropes. At different points around the circle fragile ladders dropped from platforms to the floor. As I breathed in deeply, willing the tears to go back into my eyes and not spill down my face, a figure leaped from one of the platforms onto a rope and began to descend headfirst at top speed.

It seemed to be falling out of control. I could not help gasping in terror, and I think Peter and Liane did too. The peb turned to look, not alarmed at all, more thrilled as though the display of danger was their daily bread. The figure stopped a few centimetres short of the floor.

There was a chorus of friendly jeering as the boy swung off the rope and landed on his feet.

'Ya mess dat wan up proper, Leeward!'

'Ya losin yo cool, man!'

'Wat ya mean?' the boy replied, wiping the sweat off his forehead. 'Ya try dat wan, ya mash yo cabeza in de flar!'

I could not take my eyes off him. He looked one of the oldest there. He had strong shoulders and rather short legs and his gleaming skin was the colour of milk coffee. His hair was cut like a wedge, dark brown at the roots and silvered like a porcupine's spikes on top. His eyes were cinnamon brown, with lashes as thick and dark as liquorice.

Even if Hythe had not called him the boss I would have known instantly that he was. It's called charisma, that quality that draws people to you. Up till then the only person I'd known who had it was Peter. But Leeward outshone even Peter.

His eyes swept across us. 'Wat deez niños, Hyd?' he said ironically, 'Ya bin teefin folks chilluns wan mo tyam?'

'Hey, Leeward, baby,' Hythe said. 'I'd like you to meet some special kids.' He pushed Peter and Liane forward, leaving me to one side. 'Peter, Liane, this is Leeward. He's the boss around here. He's going to get you settled in and start your training. They're yours now, boss,' he clapped Leeward on the shoulder. 'See what you can make out of them.'

Leeward looked us over, his face twisted in doubt. 'Ya wan milagro fram me,' he complained. 'Ware deez niños fram? Dey sab nada o wat?'

I could tell Peter was getting tired of being treated like an object and talked about as if he couldn't hear. 'We're Australians,' he said arrogantly, 'and I reckon we can do anything you can do!' He was eyeing Leeward off, his muscles tense, his bird-like eyes bright and hard.

A ripple of amusement and disbelief ran through the peb. The back of Peter's neck started to flush and he clenched his fists.

'Peter,' I said, warning him before he went too far. I could feel the mood of the group hardening towards us. I didn't like the feeling of being the outsiders. It made me very conscious of my white skin – and Peter's. Hayden and Sylvie had always been genuinely colour-blind. They treated everyone of any race as an individual. But I wasn't sure if this bunch of kids was going to be colour-blind towards us. I had the feeling they didn't want to like us, and that our being white was a very good reason not to.

Peter did not respond to me, but when I spoke Leeward looked away from him to me.

'Wat yo name, gal?'

His eyes met mine, curious, not cold, interested in me because, as I learned later, he studied what Hythe didn't say or do as much as what he did.

'Joella,' I replied.

He shook his head almost sorrowfully, 'Yo no acrobat, datfashor.'

All the dark eyes turned on me. I felt my face turn scarlet. I shrugged helplessly, too unsure of myself to speak.

Liane spoke for me. 'That's not Joey's fault,' she said angrily. 'She didn't want to come here. None of us did.'

She was clutching Bro Rabbit and she shook him fiercely at Leeward, making the toy's long grey ears flap and wobble.

Leeward laughed. 'Wat de hell dat?'

'That's Bro Rabbit,' Liane spat out the words at him, 'and you wanna watch out for him!'

'Bro Rabbit, hey! An yo de Tarbaby?'

Liane's face was a mask of scorn. 'You're an idiot, do you know that?'

Nothing it seemed could dampen Leeward's good humour. 'Dis gal be okay,' he said, grinning widely. 'She use dat wilness. But deez wans . . .' he gestured towards Peter and me.

Peter said again, 'I'll bet I can do whatever you can do.'

'Dis kid wanna die,' Leeward said, looking round at the rest of the peb and rolling his eyes.

'I can learn to do it then!' Peter's face was set and determined and his eyes were eager. I realised he was running on his track again, just like one of those old-fashioned clockwork trains. All you had to do was wind him up. Suggest there was something he couldn't do or that someone else could do better and he wouldn't rest until he'd excelled at it and beaten everyone else along the way.

He was being wound up now. The crowd of acrobats to compete with and impress, the tantalising equipment of the Gymna, the lure of the Galax-Arena, the sense of being the outsider up against the group, all these were like a spur to him.

'Hey, wyatt kid, ken ya do dis?' A little girl no more than eight or nine, with broad Mongolian features and hair the colour of buckskin, broke away from the group and hurtled across the floor in a complex and highly skilled pattern of tumbling. When she reached the end she stood poised and confident, her chin raised proudly.

The watching peb clapped and shouted in appreciation and she grinned wickedly before returning across the floor.

'Hey, ken ya do dis?'

'Look heah, kid, ken ya do dis?'

The Chinese girl was diving elegantly through hoops on one side. The black twins were rolling joined together across the floor. The Gymna came alive as more and more children ran to display their skills.

'Watch this, skippy!' I was surprised to hear a different accent, an English one. The speaker stepped forward. We had not noticed him before as he had been standing at the back, and he was short, though he looked fairly old, perhaps fourteen. He was the only other white person there and he had thick, long, dead straight red hair, tied back in a ponytail.

Hair just a shade lighter than Peter's. Light grey eyes, instead of reddish brown.

They were the same age and the same build. They stood and stared at each other. People talk about love at first sight, but I've always thought hate at first sight is a lot more common. That's what it was like with Peter and Allyman. They looked at each other and loathed each other.

Among the brown and black skins they made a striking pair and the chemistry that was going on made them even more striking. Hythe noticed it at once.

'Fantastic,' he said to Leeward, a note of satisfaction in his voice. 'Allyman and Peter can work together.'

'I work with Ashmaq,' Allyman replied. 'This is what we do,' he said scornfully to Peter and beckoned to a thin, dark-skinned boy who was also standing at the back. The two of them started towards the ladders, but Hythe stopped them, his right hand slightly raised.

'No, no,' he said. 'You two have been okay together, but from the colouring point of view you look sensational with Peter.'

5

Since I started writing this down I've been dreaming about Allyman. I catch sight of his face like I did on the television, and then I hear his voice coming closer and closer and I know he's after me.

This is not a fantasy because telling the truth is going to bring him after me. He'll never rest until I'm out of the way. One day I'll see the pale face and the long red hair for real. I'll hear the slow, nasal accent and it won't be a hallucination . . .

Panic chokes me up if I think of it, and if I panic I'll never get the story told. I can only take it one step at a time: word by word, sentence by sentence, I drag the story out of me. I'm not looking into the future. I'm only concerned with the past. What does the future matter, if until the past is told I'm living in limbo, neither alive nor dead?

Dis di be all is what the peb used to say. That was the way they lived – the only way anyone could live there. Life shrank down to the daily practices, the strange food that they were always hungry for, the pleasure of adorning themselves with sparkling leotards, or decorating each other's bodies with iridescent paint or sequins. Both girls and boys spent hours braiding their hair with beads, trying out new combinations of clothes and decorations, gazing narcissistically into mirrors or into each other's eyes. For us it was strange, among all the other strangeness, to be without television or books, but few of the others had known much of these before. They had other resources – games like scissor, paper and stone, cat's cradle, songs and clapping games from their own countries, stories about themselves that had become legends.

From our solitude, shut away in our one room, we now had to come out and live with the group – a group that was at best indifferent, at worst hostile, always unpredictable, a group that did not follow any of the rules that we had known before.

It took us a long time to settle in, and if it hadn't been for Bro Rabbit we would never have been anything but outsiders. The peb were not interested in new people. They were interested only in themselves. Each one of them had started off the same, orphaned, enslaved and exiled, but some became powerful and some remained weak. Sooner or later the weak disappeared, so everyone sought and hung onto anything that gave them power, no matter how small it was.

Before they were kidnapped, most of the peb were already homeless and alone. Apart from the twins we were the only people from the same family. Allyman and Ashmaq were the only close friends taken together. Two were stronger than one. Having someone else looking out for you gave you a little bit of power, enough to get the edge on someone who was completely alone. But it also made you more vulnerable. That person could hurt you, even betray you, and then you were worse off than if you had been alone to start with.

For the first few days I ached all over and every time we went back to the living quarters I fell on the floor of our alcove and slept. I was given to the twins, Mariam and Istar, to see if they could get me into some sort of shape. 'You never know,' Hythe said to them carelessly, 'the most unlikely kids can surprise you.'

Their identical faces remained unconvinced. Hythe was not serious anyway. He kept me around until he could see how much my departure would affect Liane and Peter. He didn't want anything to upset his stars. When he was reasonably sure they wouldn't be devastated, he got rid of me as quickly as possible.

Mariam and Istar were supposed to teach me warm-up exercises and basic routines, but my physical clumsiness exasperated them, and they were easily distracted into their own double act. They performed like mirror images of each other. I would sit and watch them, fascinated by their ingenuity and grace, until they forgot about me altogether, and at the end of the working period I'd made no progress at all.

The twins shrugged their shoulders and grinned guiltily at each other. 'Don worry,' Mariam said. She was both calmer and kinder than Istar. 'We keep ya heah lang lang tyam.'

But her sister rolled her eyes and laughed scornfully. She obviously didn't think I was worth wasting time on. Mariam at least showed a little curiosity about me but Istar, like the rest of the peb, made no effort to get to know me. She was completely unsentimental about it, even ruthless. She knew that I wouldn't make the grade. She knew I was disposable.

I saw very little of my brother and sister. Peter began doing floor work with Leeward and Allyman but he progressed rapidly to the ropes and trapezes, being as fearless and strong as they were and even more ambitious. Liane teamed up with Fenja, the girl with buckskin hair. They were coached by the Chinese girl, whom I had thought beautiful and who never spoke to me. She had divested herself so completely of her past no one even knew her real name. Allyman called her Precious Flower, at first derisively, later with desire, and everyone shortened this to Presh.

She guarded herself more closely than anyone I've ever known, but Allyman had some hold over her, as if giving her her name had made her his. She seemed to despise everyone else, but she was dedicated to her art of tumbling and acrobatics. Occasionally Liane and Fenja would please her and her grudging 'Wicked!' made them ecstatic.

Little by little, piecing together all I heard from the peb as they lived and squabbled, ate, slept and dreamed alongside me, and by watching, silent and unnoticed, in the Gymna while they practised, I began to get a clearer picture of the set-up Hythe had brought us into.

It was Allyman's buddy Ashmaq who gave me most information. Since Allyman had been ordered by Hythe to work with Peter, Ashmaq had time on his hands in the gymnasium. He was a graceful, deceptively indolent boy, who spoke English with the same nasal accent as Allyman, drawling the words lazily as though he despised them. He was cruel and biting in speech, but he made the others laugh, as long as his cruelty was directed at someone else. Now it was usually directed at me.

Listening to him, trying not to let him rile me, always pretending to be as slow and stupid in mind as I was in body, I gleaned little scraps of information.

The peb came from all over the world – Ashmaq himself and Allyman came from Birmingham, in England. They had both run away from home and had lived on the streets, sleeping under the motorway, staying alive by begging and by displays of acrobatics. Most of the peb had this in common: they were homeless and they were performers.

They had all had the same journey as us, the terrifying, weightless flight in the spaceship, and they had all been given the same information about where they were – the planet around the G2 star, called Vexak, – and about our new owners – the humanoid Vexa for whom we were performing animals or pets.

No one disobeyed Hythe, because most of them had tried at one stage or another in minor ways, and had felt the sickening power that came from his raised hand. There was a story, often repeated by them, of a girl from Chicago, who had defied Hythe until she went mad and died in the Gymna. No one wanted to follow her. The terror they had shared in at her death kept them obedient.

Before Leeward came (and that was 'lang lang tyam go'), they had lived in chaos. Most of them couldn't understand each other. They lived and died like animals in captivity. But Leeward had arrived and immediately taken charge. Hythe allowed it, they said, because the performances became better, but I could see how hard it would be to stop Leeward doing anything he wanted, short of killing him. His energy and his brilliance made him irresistible.

Leeward gave language of a sort back to the peb, making everyone learn patwa, so they could talk to each other at least. And he built up teams that worked together and looked out for each other.

As the peb spoke about this casually, I realised their feelings towards him were mixed. They admired him for his skill and toughness, but they also hated him for being better than they were and, even though the way he organised them made life longer and more bearable for them, they despised him for what they saw as weakness in him – a streak of idealism that made him worry about others in a group where self-preservation at any cost was the rule.

So despite his efforts to keep peace and to look after everyone, the group was shot through with intrigue and emotion. Intense friendships sprang up only to die away overnight. Loyalties changed from day to day. There were quarrels, which often led to brawls. The tension of performing and competing was deliberately fostered by Hythe. He compared each of the stars endlessly with each other, goading and challenging them to even greater acts of daring. The more reckless the peb became the more he cheered them on and, though he called Leeward 'the boss' and 'my man', he undermined him in other subtle ways.

What the Vexa liked, I learned from Ashmaq, was risk, excitement, danger. The performers wore pulse bands round their wrists and temples, and these picked up and relayed the adrenalin charge to the spectators. The greater the risk for the performer, the greater the thrill for the audience. Everything was geared to producing the most spectacular performances. The exotic, brightly coloured clothes, the decorations on body and hair all contributed – but of course by far the most important were the stunts themselves, which for a long time we only saw in rehearsal in the Gymna.

Liane's toy, Bro Rabbit, was the only thing from our former lives that survived the journey. We never saw our bags again and even our clothes were taken away. I often wonder what would have happened if that shabby grey furred puppet with the big round head, floppy ears and staring blue glass eyes had not come with us. I take Bro Rabbit out and put him on my hand, willing him to speak. He says nothing but, just as when we were there we only had to put him to our noses to smell home, now I hold him up against my face and I am transported back to the Galax-Arena.

The first of the peb actually to befriend us was Eduardo, and he did so mainly because he was fascinated by Bro Rabbit. He was very young, seven or eight I guessed, though he was as tough and aggressive as the fourteen year olds. I didn't think he had seen many toys before. He took to sitting with us in the evenings, after we had eaten. He didn't say much, and while he was awake he remained wary, but the sleepier he got the closer he wriggled up to us.

I remember one evening in particular because it was the first time I heard Peter speak in patwa. We were sitting in the entrance to our alcove, listening to the peb singing and clapping. Eduardo was curled up between me and Liane, and every now and then he would inch a little closer. But when I rested my arm gently round him, he froze, and pulled away, only to relax into my side again when he thought I didn't notice.

'Look what he's doing,' I whispered to Peter. 'He's such a little gangster when he's awake, but when he's asleep he looks like an angel.'

Peter looked down at the dozing boy as though he was

seeing him for the first time. He shook him gently. 'Hey, grommet,' he said. 'Wat ya sab bout dis place?'

The patwa made his voice sound different, as though he was no longer my brother. I looked at him closely and realised how much he had changed. The constant physical work had expelled a certain softness that he used to have. Any trace of gentleness was gone forever. He looked tough and fit, and ready for anything. He had acquired the aura of the peb. He had become a survivor.

I couldn't blame him. I would have become one too, if I had been able.

'Wat Hyd tell ya?' Eduardo countered, sleepily.

'He told us we were in some other world,' Peter replied, the patwa forsaking him. 'Inhabited by humanoids called Vexa. And that we were like performing animals to them.'

'Dat all I sab,' Eduardo said.

'Wat place ya fram?' Liane said, as though she had been speaking patwa all her life.

'Fram de ciudad.'

'Wat ciudad?'

'De big wan!'

'Wat lan dat?' Peter asked.

'I forget,' Eduardo said. 'I no lak dere. Dere, I always hungry. Heah I get plenny eat. I lak heah mo.'

'Don't you miss your family?' I said.

'Wat?'

'Yo mum and dad? Wat bout dem?'

'No mama, no papa. No familia. Nada. Jus me in de ciudad. An no food!'

He grinned at me as he said it, and stretched like a puppy. And just as I used to with Tam and Jake, I picked up a little bit of his consciousness. For a second I knew what it felt like to be Eduardo. I had a flash of the big city, but not the big city ever seen by Australian tourists. The big city of the homeless and the starving, where kids fight away dogs from the garbage so they can eat, where life on the streets is lonely and frightening and dangerous, where children are abused, stolen, murdered and no one ever knows where they have gone. No one misses them.

And then I looked around at the peb gathered in the big room and I knew instinctively that for most of them it was the same. No wonder they never referred to themselves as kids or children, except to insult each other. It was far better for them to be the peb of the Galax-Arena, even though they were exiles and slaves, even though they were used as performing animals, than to be children back on Earth.

Mariam and Istar were singing together, their voices harmonising in an atonal tune. I heard in it the sounds of Africa, ancient and mysterious. They were singing in their own language. Were they singing of the beauty of Earth and the sadness of exile, or were they, too, happy to be here where they were safe and well fed?

Tears came into my eyes. I shook them away, furious with myself for my own weakness.

'Ya lat me touch dat critter?' Eduardo said to Liane.

She drew back the hand with Bro Rabbit on sharply. 'Nah, man. Dis be wan big fierce critter. Dis be Bro Rabbit. Ya nevah, evah touch he, ya sab dat!'

Bro Rabbit's blue eyes gleamed in the half-light, making him look almost alive.

'Wicked!' Eduardo said admiringly. 'Hey, Señor Bro, I show ya samtin. I show ya segreto.'

His dark, curly hair was tied back from his face by a headband. He took it off and from within the folds drew out a tiny knife. He flourished it in our faces, with a gleeful grin. 'Señor Bro, I look afta ya,' he boasted. 'Me amigo, sab?' Then he put his finger to his lips, and hid the knife away again.

6

'E & P', Ashmaq remarked as we went down the corridor from the Gymna towards to elevator. He said it to me, talking as he usually did in English. 'Looks like someone will be heading off there soon.' Then he laughed mockingly. 'But it won't be me! And it won't be Allan!'

The twins understood enough. 'Shut it!' Mariam told him. Ashmaq had been hanging around with us all morning, needling and teasing, making Mariam and Istar laugh despite themselves.

'Yeah, cool dat,' Istar agreed, her long eyes flashing nervously.

'Dat bad luck,' Mariam told me, superstitious like all the peb. 'Dat wan puttin bad luck on ya, spikkin lak dat.'

'You don't even know what it stands for, do you?' Ashmaq whispered in my ear as we stood in the elevator. 'You don't know what E & P means, do you, white kid?'

The elevator came to its usual sickening halt. I tried to ignore him, tried to catch up with Liane who was just ahead of me with Fenja, but he was determined to tell me. As we followed the group into the living area he shouted after me, 'Experiments and Pets, that's what it means. Experiments and Pets. And that's where you're heading. That's all you're good for!'

Mariam made a little stabbing gesture with her left

hand towards him, and muttered something in her own language. 'Don worry,' she said quietly to me. 'We look out fo ya.'

But her sister thought otherwise. She told me so later, that night, after we had spent the rest of the day pretending I was improving.

'Ya cyan do dis,' she said abruptly. 'Ya never gon do dis. I finis wid ya na.'

She was rebraiding her twin's hair. Mariam sat curved in front of her, one hand bent gracefully back, beads in the palm. Istar took another bead, a deep blue one, and attached it to the dark brown hair. The two colours together were beautiful, like the eyes of a Siamese cat against its seal brown fur.

'Keep yo cabeza still, gal!' she scolded as Mariam turned her head.

'Wat dis gal gon do, den?' Mariam demanded, shaking her hair out of Istar's hand. 'We finis wid she, Hyd finis wid she.' She made a rapid throat-cutting gesture. 'Give she mo tyam, sister.'

'We be wastin tyam,' Istar replied calmly. 'Right, kid?'

I shrugged, not knowing how to answer. Of course it was true. They were wasting their time on me. I would never be a gymnast. But the alternative was too horrible to think about. To be a pet to the Vexa – aliens I hadn't even seen yet. I thought about how some people treated their pets back on Earth and shuddered.

Liane was listening from the corner, where she and Fenja were playing some game with Bro Rabbit. She sat up, Bro Rabbit on her hand, and said in alarm, 'Joey can't be sent away. She has to stay here with us. You must tell Hythe.'

Some of the others began to listen. 'Hyd got eyes in de cabeza,' Presh put in laconically. 'He sab she never gon be no good.' The sound of her voice caught Allyman's attention.

'If he don't take her as a pet, he might take you,' he said to Liane. 'You'd make a real cute little pet, now, wouldn't you?'

'Leave her alone,' I started to say, but Liane was perfectly capable of defending herself. She stood up swiftly and walked into the centre of the room. 'You're the one they should be taking. You're useless. Peter's much better than you.'

It was not true – not yet – but Peter was good. I knew he was better than anyone, except Hythe, had thought he would be, and I knew too that Allyman not only hated him, but now envied him too.

'Peter!' he spat out the name. 'He should be a pet too. Peter the pet. It's all any of you are good for. Hythe really stuffed things up when he brought you lot back. He's losing his grip.'

'Yeah!' Ashmaq bounded up from where he had been lounging gracefully beside his friend, and ran towards Liane. 'Little baby girl,' he teased, trying to tickle her. 'Little baby pet!'

Peter also leapt to his feet.

There was a sudden stillness in the room. The peb who had been busily chatting, braiding each other's hair, decorating their pulse bands, and trying on new exotic clothes, turned to look, excited and alert.

Liane spat in Ashmaq's face. He swore violently at her, and raised his hand threateningly.

Liane raised her hand too, the hand that was covered by Bro Rabbit. She brandished the toy.

'Get lost,' she said in a strange, growly voice. 'Ya de wan is gon stuff up, kid. Ya is gon stuff up real real bad. Sho bad ya is gon die!'

It should have been funny – a little girl threatening a teenage boy with a toy hand puppet. But it wasn't funny. And everyone knew it wasn't. Bro Rabbit suddenly looked grotesquely alive – more alive than Liane who had gone quiet and flat as though she was in a trance.

'Take that back,' Ashmaq said quietly. 'Unsay it. Quick!'

Bro Rabbit's ears waggled. 'Cyan be unsaid,' he growled. 'Ah has spoken. An Ah spiks ony de trus'.'

Fenja, who had been watching and listening open-mouthed, gave a sharp little laugh.

'Serve ya right, Ashcan! Ya tink ya be de boss of dis

place. Na heah com wan stronger dan ya!'

'Heah com Bro Rabbit!' the toy agreed, swaggering a little, growing larger and more important under the eyes of the fascinated peb. No one spoke. Ashmaq seemed to diminish in size. His face was the colour of ash.

'Unsay it,' he pleaded.

Bro Rabbit shook his head and waggled his ears. Liane's eyes had closed. Suddenly I was very frightened by what was happening.

I called to her sharply. 'Stop it, Liane! Wake up!' Then I said to Ashmaq, 'It's only a toy. It doesn't mean anything.'

Bro Rabbit swung to face me, his blue eyes gleaming. The voice growled at me. 'Joella don believe. Joella be wan bad chile. Dey gon tak Joella way!'

I couldn't believe it. A few moments ago Liane had been pleading for me to stay. And Liane never called me Joella – always Joey. The growling voice sounded nothing like her light, slightly accented English. I was terrified she had gone mad, that she was possessed by some horrible spirit that lurked in this alien place.

I put my hand out and touched her shoulder. She opened her eyes and said in her own voice, 'I don't want you to go, Joey, but Bro says you've got to.' Then she turned away from me and resumed the game with Fenja as though nothing had happened.

Ashmaq gave a brief laugh and shook himself. He looked round at the peb, but they would not meet his gaze. Allyman said, 'It's nothing, man, just a stupid little kid playing games.'

'Sure,' Ashmaq replied with bravado. 'It's nothing. Nothing rattles me, anyway, you know that, Allan.'

As I recall this scene, I realise for the first time that Leeward played no part in it. I replay it in my mind, but I cannot place him. So this must have been the moment when his power began to desert him, when he began to lose control of the peb. Perhaps he felt it, and that was what made him seek me out after the first performance I saw in the Galax-Arena.

That happened much sooner than I had expected. In

fact it came the following day, coinciding with the fulfilment of Bro Rabbit's prophecy about me. Istar had decided I was good for nothing but a pet but Mariam was still committed to keeping this from Hythe, and I was working away slowly and painfully under her tuition. Ashmaq, more restless and provocative than usual that morning, perched himself halfway up the wall bars and made acid comments.

'You've got no sense of movement at all, girl!' he sneered. 'No spring. What've you got in your body? Lard instead of muscle?'

Istar giggled, but Mariam got angry with him. 'Ya shut it, Ashcan! It be she fault she lak dat?'

'She built lak bus! Lak a Brummagem Corporation bus!' Ashmaq swung upside down. The patwa made him sound even more insulting. His long black hair flopped over his thin face. He put both hands up to sweep it aside, and then arched his body until it was bent like a hoop.

'Big man!' Mariam growled. 'Go way. Lat we lone!'

'Yeah, big man, that's me. Big star. I've gotta practise. I'm a star performer, don't forget. And tonight's the night! The big, big night! Dis be de noch!'

'Wat he say?' I asked Mariam, who was showing me how to lengthen the hamstring muscle in my thigh, by alternately stretching and relaxing my legs.

'Don min he,' she said. 'Ya do dis. Ya mus do dis, wan hunnerd, two hunnerd tyam.'

Istar was standing on her hands. She said, 'Ya gon see samtin dis noch. Dis noch ya see de Vexa.' She hissed the word. 'Ya see Galax-Arena live.'

She dropped back to her feet and, doing side stretches, continued, 'Ya see me an Mariam fo real. We good. We de best!'

'You wish,' Ashmaq said scornfully. 'You don't even work on los altos. Wait till you see me and Allyman and Leeward, girl. Then you'll know what your brother's getting into.'

'Peter won't perform tonight?'

'Nah, he's nowhere near ready. And if Allyman and me have anything to do with it, he won't ever perform. We work together, see, and we don't like anyone else messing that up.'

'Hyd say,' Mariam started, but she was interrupted by that smooth, friendly voice.

'What did I say, sweetheart?' Hythe had come over to our part of the Gymna, and was watching us with amusement. 'Spend more time working and less talking, I bet. Isn't that what I always say?' He put his arm round her and stroked her face.

Mariam looked down, but smiled sideways at him, pleased and embarrassed at his teasing.

'See me!' Istar cried out, wanting to get his attention. He ignored her, as he usually did, liking to keep her edgy and jealous of her sister.

'Ashcan, why're you lounging round here?' he demanded. 'You don't work with these girls.'

'You told me not to work with Allan,' Ashmaq replied sullenly, unlooping himself from the bars and dropping down to stand next to Hythe. 'You've got that new boy working with him. You know Allan and me have always worked together.'

'Yeah, I know, man!' Hythe's voice was conciliatory and kind. 'And you'll be performing together tonight. But I want Allyman and Peter to be ready to work together next time and they need a lot of practice. You get over there now. Tell Leeward to get Peter started on ropework, and you can run through your stuff with Allyman. Okay?'

He reached out and made that familiar gesture, halfway between a cuff and a caress. Ashmaq bent his head under it like a cat. If he had been a cat he would have purred. Then he gave a smile that made his cruel face beautiful, and leaped away, crossing the central space in a series of flying cartwheels and somersaults. He looked as though he had wings.

'Right, Joey, baby,' Hythe said, turning his attention to me. I stood up, so I wouldn't feel quite so small next to him. 'You reckon you can do that?'

I shook my head. He knew I couldn't. Why did he tease me?

'What do you say, Mariam?'

'She gon be real good. She jus need mo tyam,' Mariam lied bravely.

It made Hythe angry. He turned to the other twin and raised his eyebrows at her. 'What do you think, Istar?'

Istar was delighted to be spoken to. She grinned at him in her crazy way and said loudly, 'She never gon be no good. We is finis wid she.' She would not look at me. She stood on her hands again, and walked away from us.

Mariam persisted. I could only guess what it cost her to disagree with her sister and defy Hythe. 'She jus need few mo dis, Hyd.'

'Mariam, you'd better get on with your routine for tonight,' Hythe said, dismissing her. 'And, girl, it's getting real boring. Better try and jazz it up a bit. The Vexa don't like the floor work so much. They like the stuff up on los altos.'

'We don work on los altos,' Mariam said slowly. 'Istar cyan work up dere. Mak her cabeza spin.'

'You work where I tell you to work.' The same voice that had teased her before was now icy cold. He was punishing her for lying to save me. 'And if you fall, so much the better. You want me to arrange it?'

She shook her head at him, and backed away. He watched her go, raising his hand slightly. 'You do as you're told,' he called after her. 'Don't forget it. Don't any of you forget it.'

The peb, always watching him, always aware of him, heard the anger in his voice, noticed the raised hand, and gave themselves even more wholeheartedly to their practice. There was no sound in the Gymna apart from the thud of feet and brief cries of instructions. No one even glanced in my direction as Hythe turned back to me.

I only had to look at him to know what was coming. And I also knew it was what he had always intended. All the suggestions of giving me a chance, trying me out, had been play-acting. Ever since the car park in Casino when he'd meant to leave me behind but had had to take me instead, he'd had no other plan for me but to hand me over to the Vexa.

'Joey, baby,' he drawled. 'Looks like it's the end of the road for you and me, babe. No hard feelings, right? I've got a show to run here. So you'll be taking off tomorrow, honey. New life for you.'

I couldn't speak. Another separation, another loss was more than I could bear. I just nodded dumbly at him.

'You don't have to work any more today,' he went on. 'Take the rest of the day off – and you can watch the show tonight. Special treat for my special girl!' He looked sympathetically at me, and then crooked his finger. 'Come here, honey!'

Against my will, I moved slowly towards him. He stroked my head, rubbed my skull behind my ears. I couldn't help it. I leaned against him. 'Atta girl,' he crooned. 'It won't be so bad. You'll have fun.'

'You liar,' I thought. 'You bastard.' But I still leaned against him, and he went on stroking my head.

7

Practice ended after the morning session. The peb spent what remained of the 'di' preparing for the performance. Hythe had told them to rest up, but nobody could have rested in that tense, excited atmosphere. Those who were to perform were arrogant and inaccessible, like stars from another galaxy. The others were half-envious, half-sympathetic, and totally strung-out. Even I was caught up in the frenzy and forgot for a little while what awaited me the following day, while I watched the peb dress the performers. They picked out the brightest clothes, squabbled over the most glittering and exotic decorations, and painted faces and bodies with intricate patterns.

When the little troupe was ready, I was amazed at their transformation from the dull sparrows and starlings I had thought them before into gorgeous birds of paradise. But even that didn't prepare me for the transformation of the Gymna into the Galax-Arena.

Hythe led us in, performers and spectators. The Gymna looked as it always did, stark and plain. The performers stood in the centre of the floor. The rest of us were made to sit round the edge, up against the wall bars. The light was so dim we could hardly see the others. We could just catch an occasional glimmer from the sequins on their costumes and pulse bands.

'Funny sort of show.' Peter muttered, hitching himself up onto the bars and threading his arms through them. 'Where's the audience?'

'Keep your hands clear!' Hythe shouted at him. We understood why in a moment. Far above our heads the roof of the Gymna split apart. Blinding white light streamed through it. While we could still hardly see we felt the floor begin to rise.

The wall bars rose too, forming the sides of a giant cage. As the Gymna floor came level with where the ceiling had been before, it shuddered and halted. We were in a huge, glassed-in arena. Above and around us was the same sort of equipment that had been in the Gymna, but it was changed as if by magic into crystal and silver, with a chill unforgettable beauty.

While the arena was illuminated nothing outside it was visible. Leeward told me later that it was easy to forget the audience. The peb pretended they were not there. Their real audience was themselves. They did not care about the Vexa. But I was going to be given to the Vexa as a pet. I could not stop myself from trying to see through the glass walls.

There was one moment, just before the performance started, when the lights went out in the arena, and in the dimness I saw the watchers beyond.

In that brief glimpse I saw long fingers that floated like seaweed, huge heads with large, insect eyes, and lumps where ears might be. Wires connected each head to electronic equipment which ran in banks above the rows.

Insects, robots, aliens – all these words ricochetted about in my brain.

The lights came on full again and the Vexa were once more invisible, but etched on my mind was the way they sat, the way they leaned forward expectantly in their rows. They had come to watch animals perform, to be turned on by animals risking their lives. I remembered the pulse bands and what I had learned from the peb about the thrill the Vexa got from danger. Did they hope to experience death? Did the peb have to die to give them the rush they desired? Tomorrow I would belong to one of them. How would they treat me and what would they do to me? I clutched onto Liane, rigid with terror, unable even to cry.

Liane had not seen the Vexa. She was watching the performers, holding Bro Rabbit up to her face and biting into his fur. She was not terrified. She was in a state of supercharged excitement and I could feel her trembling as above our heads the spotlights gleamed dazzlingly on the silver roof of the dome, and the brilliantly decorated figures of Leeward, Allyman and Ashmaq swung into their display on los altos.

This was the first and last performance I saw in the Galax-Arena. How can I begin to describe it? I only have to close my eyes for the images to spring into my inner vision but no words can really convey the supreme skill and the outrageous daring of the peb. I'd never seen anything like it in my life and I suppose I never will again. Homeless, terrified, enslaved as I was, I forgot all that when the peb flew above the arena, defying gravity and death. I hated and feared Allyman and Ashmaq, but when I saw them together with Leeward I loved all three of them. No one, human or alien, could have helped responding to the beauty and harmony of the lighting pattern and the thrill of sudden darkness when all we could see above us were the decorations on their bodies, glowing like jewels.

After the opening display on los altos by the three boys, Mariam and Istar performed on a low glass platform suspended just above us. Their movements were precise and delicate, but the peb around us, who had been as enthralled as I was earlier, became restless.

'Boring,' Peter muttered to himself.

'How can anyone find that boring?' I argued in a whisper.

'It's not dangerous,' he whispered back. 'It's wonderful gymnastics – they're tops at it, but they're not exactly risking their lives, are they?'

I caught the slight note of scorn in his voice. I knew what he was thinking: before long it would be him up

there, performing on los altos with Leeward and
Allyman. And I thought, I won't be here to see that.

'Here comes Fenja,' Liane breathed in my ear, unaware
that my blood was turning to ice-water in my veins. I
made myself look up.

The lights changed, leaving the twins in darkness and
illuminating another platform slightly higher, where
Fenja and Presh were working with the Chinese hoops.
They slid unerringly through the rings, diving and
tumbling.

Liane gasped and Peter nodded approvingly. 'That's
better,' he said. 'It looks as if they'll go off the edge at any
moment. It gives it a bit of a kick.'

Then we all screamed as Fenja did go off the edge.
Liane hid her face in Bro Rabbit's fur. I bit my hand hard.
But Fenja was not falling, she was sliding head first down
an almost invisible rope, as we had seen Leeward do when
we first entered the Gymna. She came to an abrupt halt, a
hair's breadth from the floor, jumped down and grinned at
us before tumbling across to another rope, which she
climbed swiftly back to the top platform.

'Oh, I wish I could do that,' Liane sighed.

Eduardo was clapping his hands together. 'See dis! Na
dey play ketch wid Fenja!'

His eyes gleamed as he followed her flight through the
air. Leeward and Allyman were both catching on the
trapezes at opposite sides of the dome and Fenja literally
flew from one to the other. Her pulse bands glittered in
the lights like diamonds. Then came the darkness, and the
glitter was like jewels against black velvet. It was the most
exciting and most beautiful thing I've ever seen.

In that instant it all seemed worthwhile and full of
meaning. Everything was caught there, life and death and
everything in between. All the suffering and pain of their
lives were cancelled out by the beauty and the courage of
the performers. I understood for a moment why they put
their entire being into the performance, even though
they were being used like slaves and animals. In the
Galax-Arena they were free.

After the lights had faded, and we had descended back into the Gymna and returned to our living quarters, the peb reverted to their normal quarrelsome selves. It was late, but nobody slept. They were all high on excitement, still punchy with adrenalin.

'Now you've seen what it's like, skip,' Allyman said to Peter. 'You reckon you've got the guts for it?' His face was pale and his red hair fell loose like a curtain down his back.

'Why not, if you have?' Peter retorted. He hated not being one of the stars, having to take second place to Allyman and Ashmaq.

Hythe had accompanied us back from the Gymna, praising everyone except Mariam and Istar whom he pointedly ignored, and handing out special treats that tasted a little like chocolate. He said nothing to me, but he gave me a small piece of the chocolate and stroked my head. Mariam went to her sleeping alcove, and lay silent on her mat, but the rest of the peb were lively and chattering, squabbling over the treats, repeating the best parts of the performance, trying to outdo each other in extravagant descriptions of the evening.

I sat on the edge and watched and listened. It wasn't long since they had all been strangers to me, but now that I was faced with separation from them, they seemed like family. I couldn't imagine what my life was going to be like. It was as if after this night I wouldn't exist any more.

And nobody seemed to care one way or the other. The peb were used to kids disappearing. They all lived on the edge – while they were good in the arena they survived and if they were no good they either died under the greedy eyes of the Vexa or they were disposed of by Hythe like so much garbage. Not even Peter and Liane seemed to care. They were more interested in analysing the performances and in being accepted by the group.

'God help you when he's catching,' Ashmaq said to Fenja, gesturing at Peter. 'You'd better learn how to bounce!'

'That may be what Hythe wants,' Allyman

commented, his light eyes cold. 'A good death of a little girl to liven things up. He reckons we're getting boring. That means someone's for the high jump.'

'High drop,' Presh put in.

'Could be you, sister!' Allyman said to her. Their eyes met. His pale irises glittered. Her dark ones held no emotion at all, but some feeling leaped between the two of them. Not desire, but some sort of recognition that gave him power over her, like the power of the snake over its prey. She might run and run from him, but he would always pursue her, and he would get her in the end.

The excitement that had held me up since the performance began to seep away from me. I shivered.

Allyman stretched out his hand in a gesture that had become familiar to me. It was just like Hythe's. For a moment it looked as if Presh was going to submit to the caress, but then she jerked her head away.

'Screw ya, kid,' she said violently.

'Wrong way round, baby! Screw you! That's what you need, you uptight, kidding bitch!'

'You shut up,' Liane hissed at him. I suddenly noticed how alike she and Presh were, with their thick black hair and ivory skin. No wonder Hythe had wanted to team them up together and no wonder Liane indentified with the older girl, almost hero-worshipped her.

Eduardo and Fenja both drew closer to Liane as though they were going to protect her. But Allyman did not turn on her, as I had expected him to. Instead he gave her a careful sideways look out of his pale eyes, and said, 'Cool it! I've got no quarrel with you.'

'That's good,' she said. 'That's what Bro Rabbit likes to hear, isn't it, Bro?' She held the toy close to her face, and pretended to listen to it.

The peb watched uneasily. One by one they fell silent. Their eyes were fixed on the toy. Their attention seemed to give Bro a power he'd never had before. He was changing under my eyes from Liane's old stuffed toy into something powerful and significant, a link with life back on Earth, a transcendent and mighty being.

Once again, it scared me to death. I shook my head, trying to see him clearly. He's only a toy, I said to myself. I looked around the group, but everyone was staring at Bro Rabbit. Even Leeward gazed intently at him, a frown creasing his eyes.

'Wat he say?' Eduardo whispered, reaching out a hand towards the rabbit.

'Hip, hop hai!' came the gravelly voice, from Liane's mouth yet not from her. 'Ya gon die!'

A shudder passed through the mesmerised peb. Ashmaq leaned forward. 'Who's gonna die?' he said nervously.

The rabbit spun round quickly and shook its ears at him.

'Ashcans gon die. Ashcans gon die.'

His face blanched. No one said anything. I remembered how he had looked in the performance. His courage then made me want to help him now. 'It's only a toy!' I said again. 'You don't have to believe it.'

The rabbit turned on me. 'Joella see sho kiddin much,' it growled. 'Dey gon tak Joella way ware she gon see all tings!'

The silence grew and deepened. No one looked at me. One or two of the peb fidgeted restlessly. I suppose no one knew what to say. No one there had befriended me, apart from Mariam, who was away in her alcove. They all knew I was not really one of them. Peter and Liane had been recognised as part of their band, possessing the same awareness, speaking the same physical language. But even though I had improved more than I would ever have dreamed possible, I was still not – and never would be – a gymnast. If I was to perform I would be a liability. None of them had any trust in me.

I understood that, and I could not blame them for it. But there was something else in their downcast eyes and their secret smiles. They were glad I was being taken – glad it was me and not them. Thankful and relieved that they would survive one more day at least, one more week perhaps. Glad that they had a future, however limited, while I had none.

I felt sick with terror. I couldn't stop shivering, and still nobody looked at me. Not even Peter, not even Liane. Peter was wrapped up in his own schemes to become a star within the group, and Liane had set out on some unknown track with Bro Rabbit. Without power they would not survive, and they were both groping after some kind of power in the only ways they knew. I looked around the group helplessly and saw that they were all the same. They wanted to survive, and to survive they would do anything – and discard anyone that got in the way.

I stood up. I knew no one would try and stop me leaving. But as I turned to go to our sleeping alcove, I was aware that one person watched me. Leeward.

8

I lay down on the mat, fists clenched and eyes squeezed shut. Tears came oozing slowly onto the sacking. It wasn't Hayden and Sylvie that I thought of. It was my cat and dog, Tam and Jake, who had never done any harm to anyone, never wished anyone dead. I thought about how much I loved them and missed them.

In the background I could hear the chattering voices of the peb, sudden bursts of argument, occasional singing, all mixed up with the gravelly tones of Bro Rabbit. I had thought I would not sleep, but I must have dozed off, for the different noises all wove themselves into a sort of dream, and when I woke up they had stopped. The living quarters were quiet. Everyone seemed to be asleep.

My dream had been about Tam and Jake, and I was convinced they were still there. I felt around on the mat, sure that at any moment my fingers would find the soft, furry shape of a dog or cat, and that when I felt them their touch would break the spell I was in, and would wake me up from this nightmare, as they had from so many others in the past.

But my fingers met with nothing. This was not a dream I was going to wake up from. Hardly knowing what I was doing, I struggled to my feet. My skin was crawling. All my instincts shouted at me to get away, to run. I stumbled out of the alcove, and across the empty area beyond.

The outer doors were locked of course. The peb were shut in for the night and in theory slept from the time the main lights went off until they came on again in the 'morning' – manyan. I knew already, just from the short time we had been living among them, that many did not sleep, especially the older ones, especially the night after a performance, and that there were often people roaming around in the half-light. I'd heard intense discussion and speculation among the peb as to who they were and what they got up to.

So when I saw a figure in the middle of the area, I shrank back against the wall, afraid to be seen, afraid to be interfering in something I didn't want to know about. But the person stepped towards me and said questioningly, 'Joella?'

I knew his voice at once but I didn't want to talk to anyone, not even Leeward. I said nothing, pressing myself against the wall as if I might melt and disappear into it. He did not speak again either, until he was very close to me. Then he took my arm, just above the elbow, and whispered in my ear, 'Com wid me, gal. I wan spik wid ya.'

I had nowhere else to go and nothing else to do. In the half-light, between 'noch' and 'di', neither of which was real anyway, the living area looked like a place from a nightmare. My actions seemed only half-real too as I followed Leeward docilely into his alcove. Perhaps I was sleepwalking, perhaps the conversation that followed was all part of a dream.

Leeward hunkered down on the mat, and I sat down beside him. Immediately he whispered, 'Wat wid dis Bro Rabbit?'

'It's just a toy,' I said. 'Liane's just playing. You don't have to take it seriously.'

'Why she call it Bro Rabbit?'

'It used to be Peter's. When she came to live with us, he gave it to her. She calls it Bro, because he's her brother, that's all.'

'Strange!' he said. 'Mus mean samtin, but I no sab wat!

Ya tink it be sam kind sign?'

'Why should it mean anything?' I replied. 'It's just a little girl playing.'

'Nah, it no soun lak a lil gal wan it spik. An it spik de trus bout tings, don it?'

'It doesn't have to be the truth,' I replied. I thought he might have said something about my fate. Was he like everyone else, simply glad it wasn't him? It made me angry and disappointed too. I'd thought he might have been different from the others.

As though he was reading my mind, he put his arm round me, and said, 'I's sorry dat ya has ta go.'

It was the first kind thing anyone had said to me for days, apart from Hythe's lies. The tears came instantly into my eyes. I said in a choked voice, 'I'm frightened.'

'Don cry, Joella,' he said urgently. 'Dere samtin real importante we gotta spik bout. I bin sittin heah half de noch tinkin, I wak she, I don wak she? Samtin dat rabbit say, and samtin I seed in ya dat firs di in de Gymna. Den ya cam cross heah lak de espiritu, an I tink mus be sign.'

He fell silent. I waited for him to go on. I didn't dare open my mouth, I was trying so hard not to sob. The tears just poured silently down my face.

'Ya sees tings, doncha?' he said finally. 'I bin watchin ya. An dat rabbit spik it ta. Ya sab tings bout de peb widout dem tellin ya. True?'

'Sometimes,' I said. The tears lessened a bit. I was interested and alert as though he had woken me up. I hadn't even known that he had noticed me. But he had been watching me, and he had seen something in me that only my family had known about.

'Tell me wat ya sab bout me.'

'You're the boss here,' I said. 'You're a brilliant acrobat...'

'Not dat stuff. Everywan sab dat. Tell me de stuff ony ya sees!'

His arms were tightly round me, and his chest was wet with my tears. I'd never been that close to another person, apart from my parents. I closed my eyes and breathed in his smell as though he was Tam. And then I saw him very clearly standing on the shore. The immense ocean rolled and hissed at his feet. Behind him a huge palm tree waved fronds that encompassed the entire sky. Between the ocean and the tree was some source of wisdom and knowledge that would make me free. If only I could get to it . . .

'Wat ya see?' he demanded. I opened my eyes and almost wept again to see myself back in prison.

'I saw a tree by the ocean . . .'

'Ha!' He made a gasp of satisfaction and hugged me even tighter. 'Wicked gal! I right. Ya sees de trus.'

'What does it mean?'

'Dat ma tree. It de Ocean Tree. Wan I be lil niño, ma granny tak me ta de obeah woman. She lak ya, she see tings udder peepul don see. She tell ma granny I grow up ta be leader, grow up ta be samwan real importante. An wan I fin de Ocean Tree I sab wat to do. Sho I search de island, I walk long all de beach, lookin fo ma tree. Ma granny, she say I sab it soons I see it. But I never see it. Den de hurricane com. Granny, obeah woman, dey all die. De trees all blow dan. Ma uncle sen fo me, fram de ciudad, teach me ta juggle, an do tricks, beg, sell ganja, anyting ta mak money. An den, he sell me ta Hyd, an I en up heah. No trees, no ocean. Wat I do heah?'

'You've been a leader here,' I said slowly. 'Like I said, you're the boss here. The best. So part of what the woman said has happened.' But as I said it, I was frowning. It didn't sound quite right. It was true enough, but it was about to become untrue.

'I still searchin fo de tree.' Leeward's voice was full of grief for our planet. The vision of the Ocean Tree made me more homesick than ever.

'It might not be a real tree,' I said. 'Sometimes, with people, the pictures stand for things . . .'

'I sab dat! But I tink dis tree be real. An dat ken ony mean wan ting – dat I gon bak ta Earss. Ma Ocean Tree be on Earss, I sab dat. Sho I gotta go bak ta Earss ta fin it.'

'How can we escape from here? We're light years away from Earth!' If there was one thing I was convinced of, it was that.

'Hyd mus mak trips bak – he teef all de peb diffren

tyam, diffren place. Effan he ken get bak, we ken too.'

'But we can't get out of this place,' I said. 'The atmosphere and the pressure outside would kill us immediately.'

'I sab dat ta! Sho we need help. Hyd never gon help we, cept out de dar an inta dess. Dat leave ony de Vexa. An ya. Ya gon live wid de Vexa. Ya mus get dem ta help we. Ya mus tell dem we not animals. Tell dem dat we be de peb!'

'How can I do that?' I began shivering again. For a moment I had been caught up in the vision of the Ocean Tree. I had forgotten what would happen to me when the lights came back on again. Leeward had got right through to me with his understanding and comfort. All I wanted was to stay close to him. I felt as if we had recognised and found each other against the most incredible odds. And as soon as that had happened he was asking me to do something impossible – and anyway once I had been taken away in the morning I would never see him again.

'I no sab, gal. All I sab, ya be de wan. Effan ya cyan do it, no wan ken. Fo ya sees tings, ya don need words, ya sees tings widout words, aint dat right?'

I said nothing. I discovered things about people and animals because I knew them and watched them. I wasn't sure that there was anything psychic about it. But I had seen the Ocean Tree, without knowing much about Leeward. Was there any chance at all I could read the minds of the alien Vexa? I didn't really think there was, but Leeward believed I could do it, and that gave me a tiny glimmer of hope. I wasn't going to be taken away to be entirely passive. I would have something to try and do, something to do for Leeward.

'Joella,' he said. 'Spik samtin, gal!'

'I'll try,' I said. 'I don't think it'll work, but I'll try.'

'Dats ma gal! An try fas. We's runnin outta tyam. Look heah, I got samtin ta show ya!'

He guided my hand over to the edge of the alcove's arch.

'Ya feel dat?'

Beneath my fingers was a tiny notch. 'Yeah, I feel it!'

'Na feel dis wan! Keep yo thumb on de low wan. Feel de tap wan!'

With my hand stretched I could just get my little finger on the higher notch.

'What is it?' I said.

'Dats how much I growed. I de biggest heah na. I be too big soon.'

'What happens to you then?'

'Wat happen ta everywan wan dey get too big. Dey get disappeared! Out de dar an inta dess!'

He was still holding my hand. I gripped on to him hard. 'Don worry!' he said. 'I gonna get way. But it gotta happen soon, sab?'

'I'll do the best I can,' I said. 'I promise.'

'I's real triste ya gon. But ya gon com bak.' He let go of my hand, lifted his to touch me on the side of the face. 'No wan ever com bak,' he said softly. 'Dey all disappear inta de dark. But ya gon com bak. We gon be togedder agen.'

'Can I stay here with you for a bit?' I said.

'Yeah, stay, gal. Ya no wan be lone, na.'

We lay down on the mat, saying nothing, listening to the sleeping peb around us. I heard a sudden cry, which I thought might be Liane. She must have been having a nightmare.

'What about Peter and Liane?' I said. 'What's going to happen to them after I've gone?'

'I watch out fo dem fo ya!' Leeward muttered. 'I watch out for dat kiddin rabbit too! But no wan sab wat gon pass. Dis di be all.'

9

I suppose the peb would have been called 'children' because they were young in years, none older than fourteen. But as I have already said, the word for them was an insult, and in everything but years they were not children. For a start, they had no parents, and without parents how can there be children? Hythe was the only adult they ever saw, but Hythe was in no way their father. He was their trainer. He treated them as animals. He owned them and therefore he could do what he liked with them. Some he became more fond of than others, but that would not prevent him from discarding them once their usefulness as performers was over.

We knew he was a liar and a trickster but he looked after us, fed us, praised us, and so we felt something close to love for him. Even I clung to him when he handed me over. That is another thing I'm ashamed of. I knew with my whole being that he was evil, but I clung to his hand, and cried, and begged him to let me stay with him.

There was no dramatic parting from the others. Peter and Liane were working in the arena, and didn't even know I had gone. The living quarters were deserted when Hythe came back for me, but he unlocked one of the alcove doors that had been kept shut for a while, and brought out a sort of trolley. Huddled together on it were two very young children. They were emaciated and their eyes were shut. Telling me to follow, he wheeled the trolley to the elevator and, once inside, pressed the E & P button.

'What's wrong with them?' I said.

'No good,' Hythe said airily. 'Some turn out like that. Costs me a lot too. Lovely little dancers those two were when I spotted them, and young so they'd have lasted me a long time. But they're not going to come good, and no one's going to want them as pets.'

'Are they going to die?' I said.

Of course he lied about it. Why should he tell me the truth then when he had lied about so many other things?

'No, of course not,' he said. 'Don't you worry about them, Joey babycakes. No one's going to die. Not while your old uncle Hythe is around to fix things up, right, honey?'

It was so hard to disbelieve him when he turned on his persuasive charm. I did nothing as we left the elevator and Hythe took the trolley through an unmarked door on the outer side of the circular corridor. I said nothing when he returned without the children. These things come back to me in dreams.

On this lower level, which I now knew was labelled 'Experiments and Pets', small steel doors were set in the inner wall of the corridor. Pets on the inside. Experiments on the outside. I worked it out rapidly, feeling sick. Hythe stopped at one of the smaller, inner doors and used the card key to open it.

When he had talked about being a pet, the image that came to mind was of being a cat or a dog. But I had not taken into account the alien atmosphere of the planet. Being a pet on Vexak was more like being an axolotl. The door opened into a glass-fronted room, like a large tank. There must have been many similar tanks, but I never saw them or their occupants. There was the same constant hiss of air conditioning, strange smell and artificial light, as in the communal living quarters, but there was even less privacy. One tiled corner had taps with the same pinkish water, and the same bowl sunk in the floor for a toilet. On the front wall were two holes like portholes set in the glass. They looked just like the things scientists work through when they handle radioactive material. They made me feel horrible, like a specimen. I suspected everything about me was being monitored. I thought of all the pictures I'd seen of animal experiments and vivisection.

'Now behave yourself,' Hythe said, giving me a little slap on the back. 'Be a good pet or you'll be taken away!' As he spoke he made a gesture to something behind me on the other side of the glass. I turned round and looked at it.

That's when I clung to Hythe. Now I wish I hadn't, but I couldn't help it. I clung to him and begged him not to leave me, to do anything with me but not to leave me with the thing on the other side of the glass.

He gave me another harder slap, peeled my fingers away, and raised the bandaged hand.

'Seeya, honey!'

And he was gone. The door slid shut behind him.

I screamed and screamed, way beyond any self control. I thought I had reached the limit of grief and sorrow, but the next few days taught me that there isn't any limit. There is always the possibility of more suffering. Now my time spent with the peb seemed like paradise compared to how I felt alone in my tank prison, with the horrible thing always on the other side of the glass.

It put its long waving digits through the portholes and tried to stroke me. Its huge eyes peered at me through the glass, but how could I have read its expression, even if I had wanted to? It was completely alien to me. Had I ever shared a single thought or feeling with it? What did it know of my home on Earth? What did it understand about family or childhood?

I did not want to go close to it. I did not want to get to know it. I wanted to die so that the pain could cease.

Screaming gave way to sobbing, and even sobbing finally gave way to sleep. When I woke, I sobbed again, and slept again. I ate and drank nothing. Images floated through my mind in nightmarish fragments. I saw Peter and Allyman on los altos in the Galax-Arena. I saw someone swoop between them, and Peter swinging with his arms folded. Someone fell, and then rose again, flying with real wings. I saw Bro Rabbit, huge and grotesque, looming above a crowd of terrified peb, and I heard his gravelly voice *Hip, hop hai, ya all gon die.*

Good, I moaned to myself, We is all gon die. Mak it soon, Bro. Mak it soon.

Then I saw Leeward walking along a desolate beach. The ocean had dried up. The palm tree was dead.

Dead, dead, all dead. Voices moaned in my head. Voices of dead children, dead in exile, far from home.

Leave me alone, I raged at them, through my parched throat and my thickened tongue. You are better off dead. Stay dead and be quiet, and let me die.

But I did not die. Others died, but I did not. Maybe I wish I had, even now, because the pain of being alive when others are dead is terrible.

I lived partly because I remembered my promise. I had promised I would try to help Leeward. If that feeling I had for him of recognition and gratitude and longing to be close is love, then I loved him, and apart from my family and Aunt Jill he was the first person I had loved.

Little by little, against reason and hope, I came back from madness and death. I woke at one time in darkness with the simple realisation I was thirsty. I crawled to the tap and drank. I slept and when I woke I was hungry. There was fresh food close to me. I ate it, and slept again. The voices and the dreams left me alone. I woke again and did not recognise the arm close to my head. It was thin. I felt my face. It was bony. I did not recognise my own body. It was light and insubstantial. I realised how close I had come to dying, and I wept again, but this time at least part of the weeping was because I was grateful to be alive.

I looked towards the wall. The Vexa stood at the glass, its hands in the ports. I did not turn away from it. I just stared at it. I knew it was happy. Its fingers waved gently as though they were beckoning to me. Its eyes stared fixedly back at me. Could their expression be kind? Could it be saying, *Come here to me.*

I thought of my pets, Tam and Jake. I thought perhaps the Vexa would love me as much as I loved them. I thought of Leeward, who I loved as much as Tam and Jake, and who had asked me to help him. There's no going back, as Hythe had said – perhaps the only true thing among all the lies. In life the only direction is forward.

So I crawled forward to the glass and sat under the port holes, and the Vexa stroked my hair.

As I write this, I realise how much stroking there's been in this story, how much touching and holding. And also how many blows and slaps – the whole range of physical emotion. I suppose when you lose your language you go back to the older, animal ways of speaking. The peb spoke with their bodies, read the body language of others, used that swift instinctive observation that animals use and that humans call sixth sense.

We had a cat before we had Tam, a ginger one called Muffy. She was very affectionate and loved being stroked, but you had to be careful with her because she would suddenly get a sort of overload from the stroking and she would bite you. That's how I felt with my owner. It liked to come to the airlocks and put its long fingers through and have me come close so it could touch me. It was not an unpleasant feeling, especially if I closed my eyes so I couldn't actually see the fingers, but every now and then a wave of revulsion and shock would sweep over me, and I felt like biting. I never did bite – the thought of that scaly plastic looking skin in my mouth was too repulsive – but I would escape abruptly from the stroking, and hide away as far as possible in the corner of the room.

This was the pattern of my relationship with the Vexa. I found it horrible and repulsive, but without it I was bored and lonely. I hated being its pet, but I had promised Leeward I would try and communicate with it and so I needed to get close to it. I had no idea how to start. At first I talked to it a lot, but either it could not hear me through the glass, or the words meant no more to it than the squeaking of a mouse. I made signs at it, responded with gross overacting to its offers of food, held its hand in mine and stroked the plastic fingers. Pet toys had been provided in the tank – a couple of balls, and some wooden blocks. I played with the balls, threw them up and caught them, rolled them round the room, even juggled with them. I built towers with the blocks, knocked them down, made patterns with them. The Vexa's mask-like expression did not change.

Sometimes when I was angriest I made horrible faces and swore at it in the worst words I knew. I called it an ugly zombie, a repulsive weirdo, a cretinous freak. When none of these things brought any other response than the constant stroking, and the constant staring, I withdrew, depressed.

The worst thing about being a pet was having nothing to do. At least among the peb there had been the whole structure of training and performance. The work was hard and dangerous but it filled the day, and it gave a sort of meaning, however distorted, to our lives. I had nothing – no friends, no work, no enemies even. Just the lights going on and off, the food appearing and needing to be eaten and the visits of the Vexa, which became increasingly frustrating and irritating.

I spent a lot of time in a sort of dreamy dozing, from which I would wake not knowing where I was or who I was. If I had known then what I discovered later, I would not have thought so often that I had gone mad. I would have had something to hold onto, to give myself some sense of centre and balance. But I believed I had lost my home for ever. I thought I would never see any of my family again. I knew myself to be completely alone.

One day I woke from a deep sleep and a dream of a sunny day in the garden at home. Sylvie was weeding the herb bed and she turned to speak to me just as I woke up. I was amazed and delighted: she had come home and we were back in our old house again. When my eyes opened onto the tank walls, the sense of loss overwhelmed me utterly. What point was there in going on? I was making no progress with the Vexa. I had failed Leeward. There was no way I could help the peb. And anyway, had they helped me? They had been glad I was out of the way. They would have forgotten me by now. They had done nothing for me and I could do nothing for them. Tears rolled sluggishly down my cheeks, but I was too weary and depressed even to cry properly.

The shadow appeared at the glass, and the eyes peered through.

'Go away!' I muttered, turning my back on it.

There was a slight rustling as the fingertips scraped on the glass. It was repeated insistently.

'Leave me alone!' I said.

It would not leave me alone. It stayed there for a long time. It was awful, sitting there under those great staring eyes, being watched all day long. Finally I turned round to face it. I was going to swear at it, but its eyes caught mine and held them, and I had a flash of its consciousness.

It was brief and unclear. A skipping, a rustle of skirts and petticoats, rolling something – *a hoop? – to . . . a brother?* These were images I knew. They meant something to me. What was going through the alien mind? That it had once been a child?

I stared at it, my mouth open. There was another brief flash. Again, the impression of a child. Then, bars, locks, doors that swung shut . . . *prison?*

A child imprisoned? But that was myself. I turned away, not even really disappointed. I was not reading the Vexa at all. How stupid I was even to think I could communicate with it. It was an alien. I was just hallucinating out of my own state.

Again the fear came to me that I had gone mad. 'If only I had someone to talk to,' I said aloud. 'If only I wasn't so alone. If only I had just one friend.' I lay down on the floor, curled up like a baby, put my thumb in my mouth.

The Vexa continued to keep watch by the glass, until

the lights went out, and I fell asleep.

I woke while it was still 'night'; it seemed a long time before the lights came on again. I lay in the dark, waiting for the artificial night to end and wondering what was going on beyond my prison, in the Galax-Arena, in the planet outside. If only I had some idea of what was happening with the peb. If only I had some contact with some other human being. There was nothing I could do for myself. I was completely helpless, totally dependent on my owner for everything. I hated the feeling. The only thing I had to look forward to was the lights going on so I wouldn't be in the dark. But nothing else would ever change – light or dark I was still a prisoner for ever.

Finally the lights did come on, and almost immediately something else happened. The door in the back of the tank, which had remained closed ever since Hythe had left through it so long ago, opened. I saw Hythe beyond it in the corridor. My heart leaped in my throat with excitement and my face went hot. I called out to him, but he gave no sign that he heard me. He was pushing someone through the door into my tank.

Whoever it was was fighting him every inch of the way, until he raised his hand and under the sickening buzzing the struggling stopped. Mariam half-stumbled, half-fell into the room.

Her face was rigid with terror and grief, and her eyes were dull and glazed. She looked thinner than ever, bony and gaunt, but to me she was the most beautiful thing I had ever seen. I felt the blood rush away from my face. My heart was pounding. I thought I would faint. I reached out to her.

She looked at me for a moment before she knew who I was. 'Joella?' she said wonderingly, and then she crawled across the floor and into my arms.

We clung to each other as if we had just been rescued from the sea. Mariam was sobbing deeply and painfully, but I was almost ecstatic. To see another human being, to hold her close to me, to know that I could speak and be understood was more than I had ever hoped would happen to me again.

I wiped the tears away from her cheeks with my fingers, and ran my hands over her hair. The braids had all come adrift. I remembered how she and Istar had braided each other's hair, and my heart pounded faster, not from excitement any more but fear.

'Mariam,' I said. 'What are you doing here? And where's Istar? Where's your sister?'

Her sobs deepened to a howl. 'She dead,' she wailed. 'She fall in de arena, an die. Joella, I see her fall. She call out ta me. An I cyan help she. I cyan help she!'

'But you didn't perform up high,' I said. 'How could she die from a fall?'

'Hyd mak we go up dere. He say we borin on de flar. He say we mus work on de tap platform. Istar, she cyan stan dat. It mak she dizzy. Na she dead. I be all lone. Wat I gon do, gal? Wat I gon do? I cyan work widout she. I cyan live widout she. I wan Hyd ta kill me, put me ta sleep, but he say I gotta com an be pet.'

She looked past me and caught sight of the Vexa which had returned to its position outside the glass. She burst out sobbing and wailing. I held her close, and she rocked to and fro in my arms.

Then she started to speak again through her sobs, and I put my ear close to her mouth so I could make out the broken words.

'How ken I be pet ta dat ting? Dat ting kill ma sister. Dat ting happy wan she die. Why dey don kill me ta?'

'No, you mustn't die,' I cried, holding her tighter. 'I want you to stay here with me. I've been so lonely. I'm happy to see you here. But I'm so sorry about Istar.' Tears started to pour down my cheeks too.

Mariam shuddered. 'I mus tell ya, Joella. It was yo brudder . . .'

'Peter?' I said, chilled. 'What did Peter do?'

'He tell Hyd we borin. He say we mus work on los altos . . .'

'But why should Hythe listen to Peter?'

'Hyd lak he. He de big favourite na! An Bro Rabbit lak he ta!'

10

Now my story changes again. What follows is partly what Mariam told me in the days that we sat together in the tank, and she sobbed and talked and sobbed again, and I held her hand, wiped away her tears, and listened.

The rest of the story is made up from what the others told me afterwards and from my own inner eye. I watch it unfold inside my head as if it's on film. I don't know if it's true or not. The story is only the way I see it and it's coloured by what I am.

Sometimes I think it's too hard – too hard to relive all that nightmare and terror. Tell your own stories, I say angrily to the spirits that come to me in the night and don't let me rest. Why should I put myself into danger for you? But they answer me, they have no voice. The dead are silenced and the living are speechless. Who's going to tell their stories if I don't?

Even the ones I hated and feared – Allyman and Ashmaq, Presh, even Hythe himself, the evil as well as the good, the selfish and the kind – and not the least the ones I loved, my brother and sister – they all deserve the same treatment. Their stories must be told, by whatever means I can find, and as best I can.

When Liane comes back into the living quarters, and

finds me gone, she does not cry. If she feels any sorrow she hides it. She has just had an exhilarating work out with Fenja, and has been extravagantly praised by Hythe. And Presh has almost smiled at her and said, 'Na bad!'

Fenja has already become more important to her than I was. Liane has never had a friend like Fenja. Fenja can do all the same tricks Liane can, and teach her new ones. She also knows interesting games and chants and she keeps Liane from being lonely and bored. Fenja is tough and mercurial. She isn't afraid of anyone, not the big boys, not even Hythe. Fenja looks like Liane, with her high cheekbones and long, dark eyes. Only the hair is different. Fenja's is silvery fawn, but that means she and Liane look really striking together. Only Fenja understands about Bro Rabbit, and Fenja is the only other person Bro Rabbit speaks for.

Bro Rabbit stays close to Liane all the time. When she is practising in the Gymna, Bro Rabbit sits on the end of a pole where he can watch the peb with his bright blue eyes. When she goes back to the living quarters he is on her hand even when she is sleeping. But sometimes, because she likes Fenja so much, she lets her hold him.

In the morning she reports what Bro Rabbit has told her during the night, and the peb are both alarmed and fascinated.

'Dat rabbit sab tings,' Mariam said. 'It sab tings bout we all, dat we never tol no wan. He never tell good tings, ony de bad wans. De peb, dey skeerd by he. Dey skeerd he see dem die!'

Bro Rabbit had said I would be taken away, and so Liane was prepared for it happening. Bro Rabbit was not exactly pleased that I had gone, but he was pleased that he had been right. It was important to him to be right about things. He didn't like people who told him he was wrong.

Mariam said Bro Rabbit took over in some way from Leeward, as though one era was coming to an end and another beginning.

Leeward himself was aware of this – he knew time was running out for him and, having always lived in a world of signs and visions, he believed Bro Rabbit was more than just a toy. So he watched Bro carefully and listened seriously to everything he said.

Bro liked people who believed in him but he never seemed to like Leeward. Perhaps he thought he was being patronised. He was rude and offhand to him, and made snide comments about him behind his back. Many of the peb did not like Leeward either. They resented his leadership and were envious of his skill. I had thought them fractious and quarrelsome, but after I went they became even more divided. They also became even more competitive with each other in the arena.

Hythe encouraged this. Leeward's influence had made the teams work well together but they worked too calmly and they worked as teams, not individuals. There were fewer accidents, but there was also less danger. The time of cooperation and unity was passing. Hythe wanted more discord and more action.

I could imagine how this would have suited Peter, who had always been highly competitive and individualistic, and also lucky enough to be in the right place at the right time. He knew he was the new and rising star, and that Hythe was preparing him as a top performer. He admired Leeward for his skill, but despised him for his ideas, which he thought were naive and unrealistic. As far as Peter was concerned it was a dog-eat-dog world. Everyone had to be out for himself. That was the way things worked, and he'd be mad to be any different.

Mariam told me he was angry and depressed when I disappeared, but he told whoever would listen that his first duty was his own survival, and that he must not let grief keep him from performing well. He controlled his anger, and it put the final edge on his ability in the arena.

Like all the peb, he learns fast. Life is short, time speeds up. The hours of rigorous practice, and Hythe's amazing skill as a trainer, mean that Peter progresses rapidly.

Too rapidly, Leeward thinks, after Peter nearly slips, going through a performance routine with him and Allyman.

'Be mo careful,' he warns him, when they are back down on the ground. 'Effan ya hurt yoself, ya finis. Hyde don keep hurt peepul fo lang. Tak it easy.'

'I'm not going to take it easy.' Peter replies. 'I don't need to take it easy. I'm not scared. I can do it all. I just want to start performing as soon as possible.'

Allyman grunts. Hythe forces him to work with Peter, but he's still performing with Ashmaq and Leeward as well, and he makes no secret about which he prefers. He never loses the opportunity to taunt and humiliate Peter. His skills are greater than Peter's, and there are many tricks he can do that Peter has not even attempted yet, but Peter is so keen to learn he's snapping at his heels. The tension between them when they work together is ferocious. Instead of making things easier for each other, in the way Leeward does for whoever he is partnering, they deliberately make things harder. Their hostility is made worse by Ashmaq, whom Peter is being groomed to replace. Allyman's devotion to his friend is total. He will not admit that Peter is already a better gymnast.

'You're nowhere near ready,' he says now to Peter. 'Unless you want to do a kamikaze stunt from los altos. You'll get plenty of applause for that. Only problem is you won't hear much of it.'

'You're going to be the one that takes a dive!' Peter scoffs back. 'Ashmaq's getting worse every day. He's going to drop you right in it before long. The sooner you let me take over the better for everyone.'

'That's not true, kid,' Allyman snarls.

'Everyone knows it,' Peter says with a laugh. 'Even my little sister's toy rabbit knows it!' Then he copies Bro Rabbit's voice, and pokes Ashmaq in the chest. 'Hip, hop hai, ya gon die!'

'Don say dat!' Leeward says sharply, but Peter has seen the flash of fear in Ashmaq's eyes, and he presses after it. He has always been like that with others. As long as they're strong and stand their ground, he respects them, but once he gets a whiff of fear he pursues it until it breaks them. Ashmaq stands between him and the Galax-Arena, and Ashmaq has to go. Peter doesn't actually want Ashmaq to die, I tell myself, he just wants him out of the way. He forgets there is nowhere else for the peb to go. The only way to leave is *out de dar an inta dess.*

Peter is new to the group and he has no loyalties to any of them. He is light years away from his family's restraining influence. Not even I am there to check him. He's always been confident and daring and he's always loved to win. Now he feels totally free from anything that might hold him back. Nothing matters except to be the best performer ever seen in the Galax-Arena.

'I can say it,' he replies lightly to Leeward. 'I can say it because it's true. Ashcan's lost his nerve.' He turns to Ashmaq and flicks him on the side of the head. 'Ashcan suits you because that's where you're heading!'

Ashmaq ducks away, his dark eyes full of fear, but Allyman comes straight for Peter and slaps him round the head. Peter hits out instinctively, and connects with the other boy's cheekbone.

'Stap dat,' Leeward shouts, and pulls them apart. They're both shaking with fury.

Leeward tries to restrain Allyman, his arm round his shoulders, pleading with him. 'Don lat him get ta ya! He windin ya up. Jus cool it, na, quick!'

'Stay out of this, Leeward,' Allyman snarls back at him. 'This isn't your problem. This is strictly between me and him. I'm gonna kill him!'

He lunges at Peter again, feints as Peter responds, and kicks him hard in the leg. Peter gives a yell of rage, and throws a wild punch back. It never connects because Hythe steps silently up behind him and catches his arm.

'Careful, careful!' he says, in his lilting, soothing voice. 'You're too valuable to hurt each other.'

Allyman tries to kick Peter again, but Hythe brings his hand up lightning fast, and slaps him.

'Get back!' he growls, his voice harder and crueller now, and Allyman drops back, swearing but obedient.

All through the Gymna, the peb stop working and turn to stare silently.

Hythe raises his hand, and they all flinch away as the

buzzing starts. Ashmaq has his hands to his head. Even Peter starts to shake.

Hythe speaks to Leeward. 'You're meant to prevent this sort of thing. You losing control or what?'

Ashmaq whines, 'It's Peter's fault. He started it. He's always making trouble. You should get rid of him.'

'So you're the boss, now, are you, Ashcan?' Hythe sneers. 'Ya de big man roun heah. Ya wanna run de whole show?'

When Ashmaq does not reply, Hythe goes on. 'You can hardly run your own act. You're on the way out, kid. You get yourself together or you go, is that clear?'

'If Ashmaq goes, I go,' Allyman interrupts.

'Geez, we got another boss here! Only one person round here decides who goes, and that's me. I got other plans for you, Allan, my man. And they include working with Peter, get it?'

He raises his hand again threateningly to the three of them, keeps it there until they all drop their eyes and back away. 'That's better, kids,' he says, looking around at the peb. 'What's all this time out? What's all this loafing around. Get back to work!'

As the peb return to their routines, Hythe draws Leeward aside.

'What's going on, kid? You losing your grip?'

'Peter mak trouble,' Leeward says reluctantly. 'He an Allyman no good tagedder.'

'They are good together. They work good together and they look sensational together. Peter's a natural. He's outclassed that wimp, Ashcan, already.'

'Ashmaq an Allyman be amigos,' Leeward says. 'Dey work good cos dey be amigos.'

'This is the Galax-Arena, Leeward, baby. It's better to have enemies here than amigos. You'll survive longer that way! And the Vexa prefer watching enemies. Enemies mean energy, and the more energy, the better the show. Amigos is crap!'

Leeward does not reply, but he stares at Hythe with his cinnamon eyes.

'Don't stare at me like that, apeface,' Hythe says

threateningly. 'No one's indispensable in this set up, you should know that by now. There's a million other kids out there that's crying out to take your place.'

'Ya tink ya ken run de teams widout me?' Leeward says. 'Ya sab tings get bettah since I bin heah.'

'Better? I don't know about better. Better for you kids, perhaps, but not better for the audience. They've been telling me the shows're getting too boring. You know what that means, doncha?' Then he looks Leeward up and down and says slowly, 'You've gotten real tall, Leeward. You're a bit big for an acrobat, aincha?'

Hythe never waited for people to answer, never stayed around long enough to finish a conversation. It was part of the way he kept others off-balance and submissive. He looks abruptly away now and studies Fenja and Liane who are practising on the trapeze. Then he notices Bro Rabbit sitting on his pole.

'What's that damn toy doing there?'

Nobody answers. Nobody else dares to speak for Bro Rabbit. Bro Rabbit is Liane's and she's three metres up on the practice trapeze, swinging upside down.

Hythe pulls the toy roughly off the pole. The whole arena goes silent. Again the peb stop working and turn to stare. Liane drops from the trapeze to the ground right in front of Hythe. The empty trapeze swings on overhead, to and fro, to and fro. She holds out her hand. 'Give him back. He's mine.'

'Yeah, I know. I remember his cuddly little face. But you don't have toys in here. This is a working area. You can have it again tonight.'

Liane takes no notice of him at all. 'Give him back now,' she repeats.

Nobody quite sees how it happens. But one moment Bro Rabbit is a lifeless puppet in Hythe's hand, and the next he's back on Liane's, his ears waggling, his blue eyes snapping.

'Heyah Ah is an heyah Ah stays,' he growls in broadest patwa.

The peb laugh. Bro Rabbit's ears waggle more.

After a moment's silent surprise Hythe laughs too. 'You're one crazy kid,' he says affectionately to Liane.

It sounds as though everyone in the Gymna sighs simultaneously. It's the first time the peb have ever seen anyone disobey Hythe and not be instantly punished. In that moment Hythe loses some of his power, and Bro Rabbit gains it – the peb know it, but Hythe doesn't seem to notice.

He strides across the arena, shouting as he goes. 'That's a crappy routine, Eduardo, change it. Presh, give him some ideas. Mariam, it's still boring! Peter and Allyman, down here with me, I want to try something with you on the ropes. All of you, I want speed. I want danger. If you're scared, quit now!'

Not long after that the first of the peb died in the Gymna. She was a girl whom Fenja disliked. She would not speak patwa and so no one spoke much to her, except Eduardo who sometimes talked to her in their own language.

'She a desaparecida, lak me,' he tells Liane. 'Disappeared wan. Peepul disappear all de tyam in ma lan. Wan mo, wan less, wat de diffrence?'

Bro Rabbit, on Fenja's hand, disapproves of the girl, with her silence and her withdrawn look.

'Spik ta me, chile,' he urges. 'Ya ta kiddin proud ta spik ta me?'

She eyes him warily, then turns her back.

'Dis is wan proud proud gal,' Bro Rabbit announces. 'Dis gal gon be punissed!'

The next day the girl falls from the trapeze, hits her head and never recovers consciousness. Hythe takes her away and no one sees her again.

Bro Rabbit waggles his ears, flashes his blue eyes and throws his weight around even more. He likes the feeling of power when things happen as he predicts. I have been taken away, the South American girl has fallen and died. Hythe has not been able to banish him from the arena. He becomes more and more cocksure and arrogant.

Exile and loneliness have made most of the peb mad in

one way or another, and now this madness begins to show itself. The conflict between Peter and Allyman is stirred up by Bro Rabbit, who likes Peter and loathes Allyman and Ashmaq. And Leeward, who has always been leader and arbitrator, is depowered by Bro Rabbit, who dislikes and discounts him. The peb who listened to him before, now listen only to Liane and Fenja and Bro Rabbit.

Ashmaq is seized by panic. Bro Rabbit watches him all the time, never missing the opportunity to growl at him. 'Hip, hop hai, Ashcan's gon die!' And whatever Bro Rabbit says comes true. Everyone knows that now. Ashmaq's work in the practice sessions becomes erratic and dangerous. The others, sensing that he is doomed, begin to avoid him. Only Allyman sticks with him, apart from Leeward, who tries desperately to revive his spirit and his nerve.

'Don lat dem get ta ya,' he pleads with him one day as he pleaded to Allyman. Ashmaq has stumbled on returning to the platform from the trapeze and nearly fallen.

'It's no bloody use,' Ashmaq mutters, his face pale and sweaty. 'They've done for me. I've had it. I'm never gonna make it now. It's all over for me. That kiddin toy, and that kiddin skip. I'm finished. Well, kid them all, Hythe, and the kiddin Vexa, the whole kiddin bloody hellish place.'

He wraps his arms round his thin chest, and gazes down on the arena below. Allyman swings on the trapeze, looking back up in concern.

'Allan's the only person I've ever cared anything for,' Ashmaq says, 'What's gonna happen to him when I'm gone?'

'Ya don gotta go,' Leeward replies. 'Ya don gotta die.'

'Don't kid yourself, Leeward. We're all gonna die here, sooner or later. Out de dar an inta dess! But for me it's gonna be sooner.' Ashmaq shrugs fatalistically. 'It's after me. It's not gonna let me live. Well, I'm gonna die so full of hate and anger, it'll fry the Vexa's kiddin brains. And then I'll haunt them for ever. But you gotta look out for Allan, Leeward. You gotta protect him from that kiddin rabbit.'

'Mebbe I cyan,' Leeward says. 'Mebbe de rabbit de boss na!'

Ashmaq eyes him. 'You're on the run too, aren't you? They've got you kiddin rattled too. Poor old Leeward, poor old boy scout. You see, you got it all wrong. You wanted us to cooperate and work together, and everything would be sweetness and light. Well, quench the violins, mate. Welcome to the real world. This is how it works.' He gestures at the arena below, at Peter who is swinging on the other trapeze, at Hythe who is working on the floor with Eduardo. 'Dog eat dog, like the skip says. Everyone for himself. And no one's ever gonna get out of this place.'

'Ya got amigo,' Leeward says. 'Stay tagedder, stay cool.'

'That's just one of those little cosmic jokes that make the whole thing so much kiddin harder!' Ashmaq's face contorts and his eyes fill with tears. 'God damn it all to hell,' he mutters, and swings out over the arena.

11

On the morning of the next performance, Hythe decides to exploit the mounting tension in the group. He puts Peter in Leeward's place with Allyman and Ashmaq. Leeward argues with him in vain, saying Peter's not ready to perform, and that Allyman and Ashmaq will refuse to work with him.

'I'm tired of those two carrying on like a pair of kiddin' duchesses,' Hythe snaps back. 'What are they, top performers in the Galax-Arena, or kids at a talent contest? They work with who I say and, if they don't like it, I'll get rid of them. You know what happens then, doncha? If they're lucky they get put down, and if they're not lucky – the Vexa are great scientists, you know? Have I told you that? I think I have, heh, big boy?'

He steps forward aggressively, and Leeward can't help taking a step back.

'That's better!' Hythe croons, 'That's my man! Now, get those kids working.'

The practice session runs for longer than usual, because of Peter's inexperience and Allyman and Ashmaq's fury. Finally Leeward decides it'll be more helpful to take a break rather than continue with the routines.

The peb are supposed to rest before the performance, but this day, more than usual, nervousness and excitement prevent anyone from sleeping.

Leeward told me Peter went to his sleeping alcove alone. Liane had gone to Fenja's, where she now slept more often than not. I can imagine my brother would have preferred being alone. Perhaps he saw how much weaker the peb who had close ties with others became – how Istar weakened Mariam and Ashmaq Allyman. As soon as you had someone to care for and look after, you lost some of your own strength and power. That was the way he probably saw it. I guess the thought of the performance exhilarated him. He couldn't wait to be up there on los altos, performing for the first time, knowing what it felt like, doing the real thing at last, being one of the stars not one of the onlookers, being where he belonged.

And I imagine he would have been planning to be the best, certain he would be.

It's Allyman he's competing with now. Ashmaq he discounts. Ashmaq is finished. That's the way things work out. Life is tough, but you've got to take it on the chin, and not waste time crying over things you can't change.

Hythe knows what it's like. Hythe isn't sentimental about anything, and look at the power he has . . .

Peter is lying on his mat, eyes closed, breathing deeply – perhaps he's doing the same relaxation exercises he used to do before competitions in our earlier life. Leeward stands in the doorway for a few minutes, before Peter suddenly becomes aware he's being watched and opens his eyes.

'Ya sleepin?' Leeward says.

Peter sits up. 'Just relaxing.' He sounds totally calm, but Leeward thinks it's a front. He feels Peter is nervous, not only because of the coming performance, but also because of some other tension between the two of them. I can guess what it is: Peter admires Leeward, but he also resents him, and envies him, as he does anyone he suspects may be better at something than he is.

'Ya skeerd?' Leeward asks.

'No way!' Peter lies back, his hands behind his head.

'Lak hell! Ya aint human effan ya aint skeerd.'

'Well, I'm a bit uptight – just because it's the first time. But that makes you perform better. You need to be a bit nervous.'

Leeward nods. He doesn't say anything else, but he doesn't leave either. He lounges in the doorway, looking as if he'll stay there forever.

Finally Peter says, unfriendly, 'What do you want?'

Leeward leans against one side of the arch, and walks his feet up the other side, so he's sitting suspended in the doorway. 'I wan ya ta tak care.'

'I thought I was meant to take risks!'

'De Vexa lak it effan ya tak risks. Dat turn dem on. An mos of all, dey lak see de peb die. Sho ya tak care, ya heah? We don wan no wan dyan.'

'I'm not going to kill anyone,' Peter says. 'And I'm not planning to die. But I'm not going to be careful. You can't perform if you're thinking about being careful all the time.'

'Ya sab wat I say,' Leeward says. 'Ya watchout fo Ashmaq. Ya don lat him die.'

'Why should I watch out for him?' Peter returns. 'He'd kill me if he had half a chance.'

'Nah, Ashmaq wudnt kill anywan. He saft boy.'

'Saft?' Peter says. 'Ashcan, saft? You gotta be joking. He's the sort that'd stick a knife in your back as soon as look at you. I reckon he can look after himself.'

'Effan Ashmaq die, Allyman kill ya!' Leeward observes.

'I can look after myself, too!'

'Sho ya ken look afta yosel, man. But dat de problem. We all ken look afta oursel. Wat we got learn, is look afta de rest.'

Peter goes on the attack himself, though his voice is just as lazy and controlled as before. 'You got some sort of father complex, Leeward? You want to be the big daddy to everyone? You want everyone to love you and do what you say?'

'Nah, dat not wat I wan. I jus wan look afta de peb wan bit. I wan mak life wan bit bettah fo we all.'

'Crap,' Peter replies, 'You just want power over them. You want power as much as Hythe does, but your way is less honest. At least Hythe doesn't pretend.'

'Hyd tell lies, all de tyam.' Leeward says. 'Ya no sab dat?'

'Sure he tells lies, but he doesn't pretend to be good. You know where you are with him.'

He has closed his eyes during this speech but he opens them again when Leeward speaks urgently. 'Peter, I gotta warn ya bout samtin.'

'God, you're depressing me,' Peter groans. 'What is it now?'

'Hyd was lak we, wan tyam.'

'Wat ya mean?' Peter sits up.

'He perform heah. Den he become trainer, an go hunt peb fo de Vexa.'

'How ya sab dat?'

'He ask me ta be trainer wan tyam, befo ya com heah.'

'Why didn't you do it?'

'Wud ya do dat?'

'Well, I reckon I might. Be better than dying here.'

'Dat's why I warn ya!'

'You're mad,' Peter says. 'You could have got away!'

'Nah, de Vexa put samtin in yo arm, sho dey ken talk wid ya, an control ya.'

'They did that to Hythe?'

'Dat how he use dat hand ta control we.'

'Even so, still sounds better than dying here.'

I can just picture Peter's thought process – Leeward has been Hythe's favourite and one of the best gymnasts ever in the Galax-Arena. Everyone knows that. But Hythe isn't so fond of him any more. Peter knows Hythe likes him more. Hythe thinks he can be better than Leeward, better than anyone. If Leeward has been invited to join Hythe as a hunter, then the chances are he will be too.

Leeward says, 'Ya wud hafta hunt peb, teef dem fram

dere familia, lak Hyde teef ya all.'

'Someone's going to be doing it,' Peter replies slowly. 'If not me, someone else. Probably Allyman.'

'Ya don tink we cud all mebbe get way fram heah?'

'Get away from here? You're kidding yourself. We're never going to get away from here. We're going to live and die here. Some'll die sooner and some later. And I'm going to be later, I'm going to make sure of that.'

Without looking at Leeward Peter rolls over onto the floor and begins to do press ups. 'Catch ya later, man,' he grunts. He has done nearly a hundred before Leeward drops to the ground and walks away.

The peb are assembled on the floor of the Gymna, waiting for Hythe and the performers to join them before they make the ascent into the Galax-Arena. Eduardo is dancing with strange wild movements, snapping his fingers and chanting to himself.

Heydoo, horrodoo, makashaka, haidoo.
Marradoo, corradoo, hakkarakka, maidoo.

His eyes are unfocused and dreamy, until they fall on Bro Rabbit, sitting on Liane's hand. Then he seems to snap awake.

'Hey, Bro,' he calls. 'Señor Bro, wat gon pass dis noch?'

'Ya all watch close,' Bro growls back. 'Ya gon see samtin gran an wicked!'

Eduardo's whole body writhes with excitement. He flings himself into the dance again.

Leeward walks into the Gymna with the performers. Ashmaq is pale and tense. Allyman, pale too but with anger not fear. Peter prances in, alive with excitement, red hair and emu eyes bright and glowing.

The peb fall back towards the wall bars, as Hythe comes in. He nods when he sees the boys in their costumes, the glowing pulse bands attached. Peter and Allyman are in black and silver, Ashmaq in red.

'Excellent,' he says. 'I was right about you three. There's something about you that makes you look sensational together!'

Allyman bends and stretches to warm up his muscles, but Ashmaq stands still, shivering as though feverish.

'Don mak dem go, Hyd!' Leeward says quietly.

'What's the matter, man? You jealous because it ain't gonna be you up there? Or are you getting soft?'

'Peter not yet . . .' Leeward has no time to finish the sentence. Hythe hits him hard in the mouth.

'I'm sick of you interfering.' He speaks abruptly to the other three, 'Let's go.'

Allyman touches Ashmaq gently on the side of the face. 'Don't worry, mac. We'll be okay. We've always been okay, long as we're together, right.'

Ashmaq holds out both hands, palms up. Allyman sprinkles powdered resin on them and slaps them lightly. 'My life in your hands,' he mutters.

'My life in your hands,' Ashmaq repeats.

'I release you from all guilt.'

'I release you from all guilt.'

Then they turn reluctantly to Peter.

'Ya do dat same ting,' Leeward whispers. 'Ritual – we alway do dat.'

Peter shrugs. He holds out his palms and repeats the words. When Leeward told them to me they sent shivers down my spine. I wonder what Peter thinks as he says them. Will a gesture, a few words, really change Allyman and Ashmaq from individuals that he dislikes and mistrusts into team mates? His life is in their hands and theirs in his. But what's to stop them betraying him or him them?

Hythe crosses to the wall, and inserts the card key. The roof splits apart. The light floods in. The Gymna begins to rise.

Beyond the transparent walls the peb can briefly see the swaying heads and the huge eyes of the Vexa. But tonight they are even less interested than usual in the Vexa. They stare at the three boys climbing the ladders, their eyes dazzled as light flashes from the decorated clothes. Their hearts begin to beat in rapid unison with the beat under the pulse bands.

'Yo, skip!' Allyman shouts across to Peter. Peter gives him a thumbs up, and pulls the rope to start the trapeze swinging.

From the start it is different from any performance the peb have ever seen. It is partly that Allyman is catching instead of Leeward. Leeward is rock steady, always precisely there at the right moment, totally dependable – and with him there's also a bond, a quick glance, a grin, something warm and human that leaps between acrobat and catcher. Allyman does the same routine mechanically. Technically perfect, he shows no sign that he even recognises Peter as they swing together and apart.

The peb, watching Peter carefully because he is new and inexperienced, can tell that this irritates him. They can see him wanting to compete with Ashmaq, trying to shine at his expense, and they can see Ashmaq forced to retaliate until the actions of all three become wilder and more dangerous. There's no empathy or understanding between them, only hostility and tension.

And fear. It comes creeping into the arena. The peb feel it and huddle closer together, half-excited, half-terrified. Bro Rabbit feels it, and waggles his ears and whispers, 'Samtin gon huntin heyah. Oooh watchout, chillun!' Leeward feels it, and bites his nails, gazing helplessly upwards. The Vexa feel it, and their heads and hands wave wildly and expectantly beyond the glass.

And I see Peter pressing after it. I've seen him do that so many times, in other safer situations. He feels fearless himself, believes himself to be invulnerable. Perhaps he is almost possessed, spurred on by the shadowy figures beyond the walls, responding to their frenzy for the ultimate thrill.

Sometimes in performance the peb shouted to each other, their shrill voices echoing across the arena, but it was more usual to work in silence. So, Mariam said, Allyman's shout sounded all the more shocking. As Ashmaq flies away from him to land back on the platform, he calls to him, 'Slow down! You're taking it all too fast! Slow down, we've lost the rhythm!'

Ashmaq's eyes flicker towards him. His concentration weakens further. He stands irresolute on the platform.

Peter is on the opposite side. According to Leeward, he knows the routine backwards. As soon as they land on the platform they should take off again, leaping outwards through the glowing hoops that fall at that exact moment, and catching the ropes.

'Go! Go! Go!' he shouts, leaping out himself at that instant, and just making it through the hoop. His hands burn as he catches the rope awkwardly and slides four metres before he can slow himself.

'Leave it! Leave it!' Allyman shrieks, swinging upside down, and desperately making the arc of the swing wider as though he is trying to catch Ashmaq himself.

But Ashmaq has already jumped. Seconds too late, he hits the edge of the hoop as it falls and he falls with it. The gold of the hoop and the red of his costume turn over and over together as they plunge downwards.

Peter just catches a glimpse of his face contorted in terror and then he hears the thud as the body hits the ground. By the time he has drawn himself back up the rope Allyman has swung to the platform, and is sliding down. He walks slowly and stiffly across the floor, as if he has suddenly aged fifty years. He kneels by Ashmaq's body and strokes the black hair clumsily. Then he straightens up and looks around the arena as if he's just woken up and found himself there and has no idea what he's doing.

'Allan!' Leeward calls to him from the side, but he takes no notice. He stumbles towards the glass walls and drags himself up on the wall bars, banging against them with his head and his fists, shouting and swearing, 'You bastards! You kiddin bastards. Are you satisfied now?'

'Allan!' Another voice calls, a whisper that echoes clearly through the silenced arena. Presh approaches Allyman like a sleepwalker, her face white and set, her movements rigid. She touches him on the shoulder and he turns towards her, looking at her as though he does not recognise her.

'Com bak wid me,' she says, and takes his hand.

He follows her, tripping and stumbling, but when they get back to where the peb are still standing as though turned to stone, Hythe bars the way.

'You ain't finished,' he says. 'Get back up and finish the routine. Leeward, you take over. Got your chance after all, didn't you, pal?'

He strides into the arena and picks up Ashmaq's body. 'Peter,' he calls up. 'Get back to the platform. We'll take the rest of the routine.'

If they had gone up again and continued with the performance, Allyman would have died then. He was ready to kill himself through grief and rage. And if Bro Rabbit had not interrupted and Allyman had died, I would not still be looking over my shoulder at least once a day and thinking I see him. I would not wake in the night and dream he is there. But who knows who would have survived that night? Probably none of them, for none of them was capable of performing, and if they had not survived that night then I would not be telling this story now.

Total silence, Mariam told me, followed Hythe's command. It's obvious to everyone that Allyman cannot go on. And none of the peb wants to go on with him, fearing what his grief will do to them. But, as always, because they are not free, they look at their trainer. They study Hythe. They read anger in him, but they see more than that. They see the pleasure behind the anger. They know Hythe desired Ashmaq's death because it gratifies the Vexa. And they are terrified he will sooner or later desire their own. The same fear that came creeping into the arena and snatched Ashmaq away, now paralyses them.

Bro Rabbit speaks for them. This is why they love and

admire him. He speaks when no one else dares to speak, and he says what no one else dares to say. Liane steps out in front of Hythe and Bro Rabbit says, 'Wan dess fo wan di. Nudder di, nudder dess. We see gran stuff na – we see de wicked gals!'

She takes the toy off her hand and gives it to Eduardo to hold. Then she and Fenja run to the ropes and begin to climb them.

Eduardo gives a shout of pleasure, and resumes his wild dancing and chanting, with Bro Rabbit flapping and waggling on his hand. One by one, hesitantly, the peb take up the sound. The arena echoes with it. It is quite unlike any other routine anyone has seen, Mariam said. Liane and Fenja swing from trapeze to platform and back again, as if they are in a playground. In the face of captivity, exile and death itself, they spin and fly in the Galax-Arena, while below them the peb dance and chant, most with tears in their eyes as they weep for Ashmaq, and for themselves.

12

Nudder di, nudder dess, Bro Rabbit had said, and he was right. The next one to die was Istar.

Liane was as shocked by this as anyone. She didn't like Ashmaq or Allyman so it was no suprise to her that Bro Rabbit didn't like them either. But she had no quarrel with the twins. She often helped them braid their hair and decorate their faces and bodies for performances. She liked to hear about their life back on Earth, and she loved the desert stories and songs they told her.

If anything, Istar was her favourite for Istar's streak of wildness appealed to her.

Was this why Bro Rabbit spoke through Fenja to predict Istar's death? Was Fenja jealous of Liane's friendship with the twins? Or had Bro Rabbit by this time broken away from them and become a real spiritual being, with true insight and power?

Impossible to know. Bro Rabbit never speaks now, and Liane pretends he never did. As I've said before, the peb were all more or less insane. Perhaps Bro Rabbit was only a mouthpiece for their dark side. He put into words what they felt but didn't dare say, and what they felt most often was: let whoever die, as long as it is not me!

The frenzy that built up to Ashmaq's death didn't go

away after it. It became wilder and more dangerous. Allyman blamed Peter, and Peter too might have blamed himself. But he always hated being made to feel guilty; he would have acted angry instead. The hatred between the two of them was not a simple thing, involving only them. It spread over everyone, forcing them to take sides. And the factions were not divided equally. Loyalties and friendships crossed all sorts of lines. Only Leeward remained apart from them, and he found that, in trying to stay friends with everyone, he ended up friends with none.

Bro Rabbit liked Peter and hated Allyman. But Liane and Fenja, when Bro Rabbit was not speaking through them, adored Presh, and after Ashmaq's death Presh supported Allyman with a fanatic loyalty.

Eduardo, who hung on every word Bro Rabbit said, and was now allowed to hold him when he was just a limp, floppy toy, mistrusted both Peter and Allyman, while Presh despised Eduardo, and only spoke to him to criticise him.

And through all these shifting intrigues and emotions moved Hythe, the trainer, calming some with a smile and a caress, and inciting others to fury and panic with harsh words and blows.

Mariam and Istar, in particular, came in for his scorn. At one time they had been favourites, but now he decided their routine was boring and he started looking for ways to liven it up. During rehearsal one day in the Gymna, he told Liane to work with them.

'Look as if you're throwing her to each other,' he said. 'Try it on the floor, and then you can take it up on los altos.'

Istar was walking on her hands. She flipped herself upright, fixing Hythe with her long, manic eyes.

'We don work up dere,' she said.

'You work where I say, girl.'

'We ken try it,' Mariam said soothingly.

Istar looked up and shook her head. 'Ta high!' She giggled and fluttered her eyelashes, circling Hythe rapidly to keep out of the way of his hand.

'Istar,' Mariam pleaded, whispering to her in their own language.

Liane waited impatiently between them. 'Let's get started,' she snapped.

Fenja watched from the side, Bro Rabbit on her hand. Istar would not stop fooling around, as if she was trying to mask her fear with this show of idiocy.

'Dat is wan fool gal,' Bro Rabbit commented suddenly. 'Dat gal gotta go. She too big fool fo dis place.'

As usual when Bro Rabbit spoke, silence fell and all eyes turned to him. Only Istar did not hear. She went on giggling and spinning.

'Okay,' Mariam said to Liane, trying to ignore Bro's words. 'We work na.' But Istar spun and giggled and spun, deaf to her sister as well.

Hythe slapped out at her; his hand connected with her head. She stopped and held her hands to her face. Tears came as freely and as wildly as the laughter.

'Shush, shush,' Mariam said, holding her close. 'Don cry, sister.'

'Ya cry, gal!' said Bro Rabbit. 'Ya cry, Istar, cos ya be finis!'

This time Istar heard. She turned her tear-stained face towards Fenja. 'Wat he say?'

'Istar be crazy! Istar be finis! Istar gon die,' the voice growled triumphantly.

'An it true!' Mariam turned her face to me, and for a moment I saw her dead sister there. 'She wen crazy wan she on los altos, an she fall an die.'

I felt sick with guilt and grief. It was my family's fault that Istar was dead. Peter had thought the twins' work was boring and had told Hythe so. And Liane had let loose who knew what implacable spirit in the form of Bro Rabbit. And if they were guilty then I must be guilty too.

There was nothing I could do or say to make Mariam feel better. Nothing would change the fact that Istar was dead, gone for ever. Nothing would bring her back.

Nothing would bring Ashmaq back either, nor all the

others who had died in the Galax-Arena. And there was no way any of us would ever get home again. After Mariam's story there was no space left for even the smallest fragment of hope. Leeward whom I had trusted and loved was no longer in control of the peb. The dreams he had shared with me had no significance – they were just lunatic ravings. I had not been able to talk to the Vexa in any way, nor would I ever be able to.

I'd been overjoyed to see Mariam; I'd thought I could bear things if only I had someone with me, but now she was there I felt worse. Her company and friendship came with a high price; I was afraid I was going to have to watch her fade and die. I would survive her, and carry the burden of grief for her as well as all my other grief and guilt.

Her story had taken several days to tell. She would talk rapidly, for some time, and then withdraw into a silent and terrible world of her own. Sometimes she dozed, and then I slept too, but she would awaken with a cry of terror, looking around her with wild deer eyes. Then she would talk feverishly again, going over and over the same things, holding my hand, looking deep into my eyes, as though I could reassure her that there was still some meaning in our lives.

But I couldn't reassure her. For it seemed to me now that there was no meaning, no meaning at all. There was nothing but madness, incoherence, random evil. Can beasts in the abattoir understand the meaning of their lives? Can they communicate in any way with their slaughterers? If the meatworkers could truly hear the animals, could read their cries of fear and understand their panic, they would not be able to kill them. If the Vexa had understood us, they would not have been able to keep us like animals. They would have set us free. But they could not understand. They were even more removed from us than we are from animals. For at least we and the animals share the same planet. The Vexa were totally alien.

Mariam's story was also interrupted by our Vexa owner who came many times to visit us. Mariam hated it. She would not look at it. She crawled to the back of the cage and hid her face, and she would not eat or drink while it was there. I did not want to go near it, but it was hard to ignore. It gazed persistently in through the glass, put its hands through the portholes to try and touch me, and brought endless titbits of food that it thought might tempt us.

It's hard to describe the next part of my story. For I can't quite remember which insight came first. There were many little things that suddenly added up to the whole picture and, of course, once I had seen it, I couldn't understand how I had missed it before.

I said earlier that we didn't exactly forget our parents but that we drew a curtain over that part of our lives and started again. That was true for me while I was still living with the peb but, since I had been on my own as the Vexa's pet, I had been dreaming and daydreaming constantly about my life at home. I often heard my parents' voices. I woke to the sound of Sylvie calling my name, or Hayden explaining something in his slow, careful way. One morning I lay dozing next to Mariam, listening inside my head to Hayden arguing with Peter about science fiction. Hayden was sounding typically sceptical and he kept repeating one phrase, *blinding them with fake science*.

They were nothing alike, but in my dreamy state Hayden kept merging with Hythe. And then it was Hythe's voice I heard. *Blinding them with fake science.*

Then there was the child with the hoop. The image I had received from the Vexa would not go away. I dreamed about the child, and sometimes she was me, and sometimes she was someone else . . .

Mariam had been brought to the tank right after I had said I was lonely and wanted someone to talk to . . .

Did my owner understand me after all? Could it hear the sounds we made through the glass walls of the cage and did it understand our speech?

I suppose all these things lay unconnected in my subconscious mind until one tiny last element appeared, and everything else fell into place.

The Vexa had just fed us and I was trying to persuade Mariam to eat something when I was distracted by a sound long unheard, but familiar, completely earthlike, so unlike everything else in that alien place that for a moment I couldn't believe I was really hearing it. I thought it was another hallucination, a buzzing in my ear, a horrible echo of Hythe's raised hand. I pulled at my ears, but the buzzing didn't go away.

I looked around the tank, searching for the source of the sound. It stopped, and I turned back to Mariam with a shrug. But almost immediately it started up again. Something came buzzing towards me, brushed past my face, and landed on the food.

It was a fly.

Nonchalantly it cleaned its feet.

I stared at it utterly dumbfounded.

It looked just like an ordinary fly from Earth. I wondered stupidly if the Vexa had flies, if the fly was common throughout the universe, but then I realised that if it were a Vexan fly it would not survive inside the false atmosphere of the tank. If what Hythe had told us was true it would drop dead in a few seconds.

It gave no sign of dropping dead. It was a very healthy fly and it did not seem to think it was light years away from Earth. It cleaned its feet, sucked at the food, and took off again. It cruised round the tank as if it was in our house back home. I could not take my eyes off it. It was the most stupefying thing I'd ever seen.

If what Hythe had told us was true ... but when had Hythe ever told the truth? I knew he lied about everything always. How come I'd been taken in by the greatest lie of all?

And then I remembered the look on his face, as we walked down the corridor for the first time towards the Gymna, when Peter had told Liane about relativity and gravity. I knew now what that look had been saying. *Sucked in*, it said, *Sucked in*.

Mariam had dozed off again while I was staring at the fly. I grabbed her arm and shook her violently awake.

'Mariam,' I said. 'Mariam, listen to me!'

'Leave me lone, Joella, I cyan eat.'

'Wake up, Mariam. Look, look at this!'

She opened her eyes. 'Wat?'

'There's a fly in here.'

'Wat?'

'There's a fly in here. A fly from Earth.'

She stared at me, not knowing the word, not understanding.

'Don't you see what it means?'

When she shook her head, the words burst out of me as though they knew they were true. 'Mariam, it means we could be still on Earth.'

'Joey,' she begged me, 'Don ya go crazy ta, gal!'

I felt as if I was going crazy – partly from hope, flooding back through me, and partly from a shattering sense of disorientation. Who were the Vexa if not aliens and where exactly were we if not on some other planet? Had I gone completely insane, or had I just, finally, come to my senses? I felt literally sick as the whole false world wavered around me.

Through the nausea one thing stood out clear: if we were still on Earth, escape had become possible.

I looked round the tank. It did not offer any immediate way out. The only openings were the door through which Hythe had brought first me and then Mariam, and the portholes through which the Vexa put its hands.

The portholes, and all they stood for, made me feel sicker. What extraordinary lengths someone had gone to, to make sure we were taken in by the deception – the fake rocket trip, the elaborate structure of the Gymna and the Galax-Arena, the pink water, the weird food, the . . . *costumes* worn by the Vexa – all this so the peb could be convinced they were on some other planet and had no hope of escape. I remembered Hythe saying the Vexa were so great at terraforming. They hadn't built a fake Earth for their performing animals. Someone else had built a fake alien planet. And not for animals. For *children*.

So who was it? It could not be only Hythe. Others, many others, must be involved. The Galax-Arena was enormous – who would be able to afford a set-up like that. And why? Why?

I cracked my hand against the glass in rage. It was glass of a sort, though before I'd thought it was some kind of alien plastic, because that was what I'd expected it to be. My rage grew as I realised how much we'd all cooperated in our own deception. Why hadn't any of us realised before? We'd been blinded by fake science, just as Hayden had said.

The rage gave me an energy I hadn't felt for ages. I couldn't wait to confront my owner. It must be human. I had shared a fragment of its consciousness. It had been a child. It could most probably understand everything I said to it. It cared about me. I was going to use that. I was going to make it do what I wanted.

If it was my owner it had responsibilities to me.

When it came to the glass again, I walked straight up to it. It put its strange fingers through the porthole. I did not flinch away from it. Mariam watched open-mouthed and shuddering as I stroked and caressed its hands. I found what I was looking for quite quickly. There was a velcro-type fastener on the forearm just above the wrist. Looking straight into the eyes of the Vexa I undid the fastener and drew off the glove. It could have taken its hands out but it didn't.

Underneath was a human hand, very thin and frail, with liver-coloured spots on it, the hand of an old, old person.

'You can understand me, can't you?' I said to it, speaking close to the porthole. 'You are a person, aren't you?'

It pulled its hands back, and I let go. The glove fell to the ground inside the tank. With one alien and one human hand the Vexa slowly removed its mask. The huge eyes and the waving tentacles slid away. Below was an ancient face, and almost hairless skull, and two small, bloodshot eyes. It was impossible to tell if it was a man or a woman, but it was a human being.

It looked fearfully around and then put its thin old lips close to the porthole and spoke in a faint whisper.

'Once I was a little girl like you!'

13

'Ya bitch!' Mariam saw what it meant immediately, just as I had done before. If we were still on Earth, we had a chance of escape, but if we were still on Earth the beings that had captured and enslaved and murdered the peb were not alien but human.

I heard in Mariam's voice all the rage I was feeling. She struggled weakly to her feet and crossed the tank to the portholes.

'Ya bitch!' she said again clearly.

The old, old eyes began to water. The old head wobbled from side to side. The cracked old voice whispered, 'I'm sorry, I'm sorry!'

'Why ya do deez tings?' Mariam's voice was breaking with outrage and anger. 'Why ya treat we dis way?'

The ancient person looked quickly up and down the corridor beyond the glass. Then it whispered again rapidly, 'I will tell you everything. I'll explain it all. I want to help you.'

'Don believe she,' Mariam said to me. 'It sam udder trick. Heah be all lies, nada but lies, lies and wickedness and dess.'

'I know you have been very badly treated,' it said. 'I'm very sorry. I didn't realise . . . I want to put things right. I want to help you!'

Mariam spat at the glass and retreated towards the back of the tank. I felt like doing the same. The person's words meant little to us. How could the deception and the brutality we had suffered be 'put right'? What stupid platitudes was this human monster mouthing because it felt 'sorry'? I liked it even less now than I had when it was a Vexa. But it was my only link with the real world and it had the power of life and death over me.

'How can you help us?' I said slowly.

The old person gave us a weak smile. 'I don't know exactly how. But I'm sure we can think of something.'

'What is this place?' I said urgently. 'What's happening here? Who runs it? What's it all for? Why did they have to pretend we were in Space?'

There were so many things I needed to find out, but I didn't even know if I was asking the right questions. And my shocked mind kept losing hold of the fact that everything I had believed before must now be untrue. Then I would think – maybe Hythe had not been telling lies; maybe his story was true after all and the creature in front of me really was a Vexa and was telling me lies now.

For the story the old person told me was far stranger and far more horrible than Hythe's fabrication of the distant planet of Vexak and the Galax-Arena.

Her name was Emmeline Carson. She was very old and she had been very rich. That was what all the Vexa were – old, rich people who wanted to live for ever. They had joined a secret project called Genesis Five which was researching immortality. Enormous amounts of money had been given to the project – enough to kidnap who knows how many peb, enough to build dozens of fake spaceships and Galax-Arenas.

The researchers had started using all the usual techniques: diet and exercise, massive injections of vitamins, deep sleep therapy, low temperature therapy, drug therapy. More or less by mistake they had stumbled on the idea of stimulating the adrenalin glands.

'It seemed truly to promise cell regeneration,' Emmeline said reverently. 'Imagine, never having to die!'

Then the team came up with the theory that they could use old childhood patterns in the brain. If the adrenalin glands could be stimulated in the right way – for instance by creating dangerous situations involving children – and if the children's reactions of excitement and fear could be transmitted into the brains of the old, the body might be fooled into thinking it was still a child's body, and slow down or even reverse its own aging process.

'Din slow it dan much fo ya!' Mariam commented, disbelieving. We were huddled side by side in front of one of the portholes, whispering through them to Emmeline.

'How old do you think I am?' Emmeline asked her.

'I no sab, eighty, ninety mebbe.'

'I'm one hundred and nineteen! And I'm one of the youngest here.'

'So it works?' I said.

'Yes, my dear, it works. It's a remarkable discovery. To think, people can live – who knows how long! Maybe forever!'

'But other people die so you can live,' I said. 'Why should they have to die?'

'That worried me,' Emmeline admitted, in her creaky old voice, her eyes moist with tears. 'When the children started dying, I didn't think that was right. And to tell you the truth, I've never really been quite happy with the death transmissions – even though they work better than anything. It's quite amazing, I suppose – you see, you actually experience death – and then you find you are still alive. You are training your body never to die. But it upset me ...' her voice nearly faded away altogether, but then her face brightened as she thought of something else. 'Though the doctors said the children liked performing and taking risks. They told us they enjoyed the danger and that they were very well treated. And they said they had all come from very sad backgrounds where they would have died anyway. At least they had some happy times here.'

I could not speak, thinking of the Galax-Arena. No

wonder the peb used 'kid' and 'chile' as swear words.

Mariam hissed, 'Is not "dey". Is "we". We is de *chillun* ya spikkin of! Ma own sister die cos of ya an yo doctors!'

'I never really wanted anyone to die,' Emmeline said nervously. 'I'm really sorry, my dear.'

'Sorry!' Mariam muttered, her shoulders hunched in despair. I could feel her breath on my face, heavy like sobbing.

'What about the ones who are kept as pets?' I said. 'What about me and Mariam? What good are we to you?'

'Oh, my dear, you've been a huge amount of good to me. That's partly why I want to help you, because I'm so grateful to you. I was being awfully silly before. I didn't want to go on with it any more, you see.'

'Go on with what?'

'With the project. I know they keep telling us the death experiences are so good for us, but I didn't like them. And I was tired of the whole thing. It's been going on a long, long time. It all seemed worth it when we started. But now, what I want more than anything else is just to go outside. And, well, I wasn't sure I wanted to live for ever after all. My family have all been gone for years and I haven't really got any friends here.'

Tears began to run down her cheeks again.

'Go on,' I prompted her.

'So they said I could have a little child of my own to look after. A lot of us do, you know. It's another experiment. We aren't supposed to talk to you – you're meant to think you're still on the other planet, otherwise you might try to run away, but we can stroke you, and bring you little bits of food to eat. And when I saw you, you were so very sweet, such a dear little pet. You reminded me of a little dog I had when I was a girl, Clover, my Sealyham terrier. Just the same eyes and the same dear face. Clover had to be put down in the end, and I cried my eyes out . . .' She had to stop because she was crying so much now remembering it.

I couldn't believe Emmeline was crying over a dog that had been dead for over a hundred years; it made me think that perhaps she did care for us, her new pets – but did she care enough to let us out? I wanted her to keep talking. I wondered if she talked to anyone else in that weird place. What on earth would they talk about? She was lonely, that was clear. I wanted to make her see we were people, so she would have to help us. 'Don't cry,' I said. 'Tell us some more. Did I do you any good?'

'You made me want to start living again. I had to live to look after you. But I thought you were going to die. I knew you were lonely, so I suggested they find a friend to keep you company . . . but when your friend came, I was frightened when I saw her. She looked so like one of the performers who died, I thought she was a ghost. That upset me very much.'

'That was her sister,' I said. 'Her twin.'

Emmeline put her hand up to her face and rubbed her eyes. 'It's wrong,' she said in a low voice. 'I won't do it any more, it's wrong.' She looked at Mariam, silent and despairing, and said to me, 'She reminds me of a bird my brother caught. He kept it in a cage, but it was never tamed. It was frightened of people, and when the wild birds flew past outside it would call desperately to them. In the end it refused to eat or drink, and died.'

'Mariam will die unless you let us out,' I said.

Emmeline nodded. 'Yes, that's what I'm afraid of. But I don't know if I should let you out. They'll all be so angry with me . . .' her voice broke off.

'You're as much a prisoner as we are, aren't you?'

She said nothing for a few moments. Her eyes went blank as though her mind was wandering. Then she said, 'Oh no, I'm not a prisoner. Of course not. I'm a share-holder in Project Genesis Five. We all are. It belongs to us. Look, they give us keys to everywhere – we can come and go as freely as we like, except we aren't allowed to go outside of course.'

She smiled but it sounded just as though she was quoting some propaganda she'd had spouted at her too many times.

'Ya a prisoner,' Mariam said. 'She cyan help we, Joella.

She wan foolis ol woman! Na good fo nada.'

Emmeline stared at Mariam. 'She came back,' she muttered. Now I was convinced her mind was wandering. She'd forgotten I'd told her Mariam was Istar's twin.

'The one that died came back. This time, I'll do something. I won't let her die.'

'Then you've got to let us out,' I said. Her remorse was the only power I had over her and I was going to use it. 'It was your fault she died, but now you've got a chance to put it right. You can save her life now.'

'Tell me what to do,' she said, in a little childish voice.

I could see the card keys in her hand. 'Can you let us out of the door at the back? Do you have the keys to the elevators and the Gymna?'

'Yes,' she replied. 'Yes, I do. Yes.'

14

'Don trus she,' Mariam hissed in my ear. 'Ya cyan sab wat pass outside de dar. *Out de dar an inta dess.* Ya heerd de peb say dat.'

'If we stay here, we die, anyway,' I replied, trying to think fast and talk slow. I was almost certain Emmeline was not lying to us, but after the lies we had already been told, who could be certain of anything? I thought Emmeline was foolish, as Mariam said, and timid and sentimental too. I wondered why anyone would have thought she deserved to live forever. But there was no one else who could help us. We had to trust her.

'Open the door for us now,' I said. I had a terrible sense of urgency. I knew we would not remain undiscovered for long. At any moment the door might open itself and Hythe would be on the other side of it. *Out de dar an inta dess . . .*

'Does it have to be right away?' Emmeline said pleadingly. 'It's so nice having you here. I've got so fond of you. You'll be safe here. It'll all be our secret and I'll look after you. No one will hurt you while I'm here.'

Mariam and I looked at each other. I knew she felt the same as I did – better to be dead than to stay in the tank being Emmeline's pets and knowing we were still on Earth.

'Effan we get out, ya ken com wid we,' Mariam said. 'Ya see de outside, lak ya say ya wan.'

'But if I leave the Project I might die,' Emmeline said. 'And I'm . . . I'm afraid of dying.'

'Everywan gon die,' Mariam replied, sombre. 'De ol gotta die, so de young ken live.'

'I would have liked to have children,' Emmeline said, rambling again. 'Then I would be leaving something behind.'

'You have children,' I argued, trying not to choke over the word. 'You have us, and all the other peb. We'll be your children!'

Emmeline stood trembling, doing nothing. I was seized by panic that the decision was going to be too hard for her to make. She would just go on and on hesitating, playing with the idea of letting us out, but never actually doing it. We would be trapped in the tank for ever, knowing what we knew, until they came to put us to sleep for knowing too much.

'Look at her,' I said, turning Mariam's face towards Emmeline. 'You can save her this time. And think of your dog. Remember Clover. You couldn't save her, but you can save us. If you don't let us out we'll be put to sleep, just like Clover.'

The thought of her old dog made her smile fondly. 'You're right, dear,' she murmured. 'I must let you out. Just let me pat you for a minute.' She put her ungloved hand back through the porthole and touched my face. I rubbed against it like a dog. I would have done anything at that moment to persuade her to go to the controls.

'Good girl,' she said.

'Do it now!' I urged her.

Mariam said abruptly, 'Wat bout dat lif ting? She gon work dat for we ta?'

'Meet us at the elevator,' I told Emmeline, adding swiftly, 'Clover needs you to take her outside.'

'I'll do that,' she promised. 'Wait for me, little Clover.'

She gave me one last pat, and withdrew her hand from the porthole. She disappeared from our sight, and a few seconds later the door of the tank slid soundlessly open. Mariam and I gazed at it for a couple of seconds. Then we grabbed hands and scrambled through it.

The corridor outside was empty, all the doors closed. I remembered the two small children I had last seen disappearing behind one of those doors. I wondered what went on there. I would have believed anything of the people running Project Genesis Five. But there was nothing I could do for them now. I didn't honestly think Mariam and I could save ourselves, even with Emmeline's help. My one hope was to get back to the peb, to get to Leeward and tell him our incredible discovery. Together perhaps we had a chance of getting away.

I had been in the tank for so long I was stiff and clumsy. I could hardly move my legs to follow Mariam. I staggered and put my hand out onto the curved wall of the passage, felt the faint vibration that Hythe had told us was spinning, and felt rage rise in me like spew and choke me. I would kill him for what he had done to us and to the rest of the peb. The rage gave me energy, made my muscles work again. I caught up with Mariam just before the elevator. There was no sign of Emmeline.

Mariam was pressing the call button frantically, but without the card key it would not respond. 'Na good,' she said savagely. 'I tol ya we cyan trus dat ol bitch!'

We heard a distant ping, a slight humming.

'It's coming down,' I said.

'Den samwan com dan innit, cos we cyan mak it work!'

The humming stopped. The elevator doors opened. It was empty. But on the floor lay the cluster of card keys that I had last seen in the old woman's hands.

'Muddah!' Mariam groaned. 'Ware she gan? She set de trap fo we!'

'Come on,' I pulled her into the elevator, scooping up the keys. What had happened to Emmeline? Had she chickened out? Or had she been discovered? Surely nothing could go unobserved in this nightmare place where the powerful knew everything and the powerless nothing. Why had she left the keys for us? Was it her who'd left them? Was it to help us get out, or was it to lead us into another trap. I couldn't think straight. There was just one idea in my head which was to get to see Leeward again before I died.

I inserted the cards one after the other. The third or fourth one closed the elevator doors. 'Where will the peb be?' I said. 'What time of day is it?'

'We try de Gymna firs,' Mariam said, pressing the button. 'It still be manyan, di tyam.'

I remembered the food I had eaten earlier. It had been the first meal of the day. I remembered the fly, the alien that had turned into a pathetic old woman. How could so much have happened and it still be manyan?

Once again the enormity of the deception swept over me, making me mad with rage, giving me energy and purpose. I would fix those bastards whoever they were. I would kill them!

The elevator stopped and we stepped out cautiously. The corridor was empty.

My hands shook as I tried the card keys outside the Gymna. The doors slid apart. In my rage I wanted Hythe to be there. I wanted to confront and accuse him. But as soon as we entered, I sensed his absence. Only the peb, in their dull practice clothes, were there, scattered throughout the area. I remembered vividly the first time I'd seen them – birds in an aviary, I had thought them – but this time they did not fly chattering towards us.

As the doors opened they turned casually to see who it was, as they always did, eager for any diversion from the monotony of rehearsal. Then one by one they froze, staring at us. No one who had been taken away had ever come back. We must have seemed like ghosts.

Leeward was the first to approach us. He looked different. He was taller and he had changed in other ways. His cinnamon eyes glowed with a curious, feverish light, like a hunted animal. When we first saw him, he had been the boss, brilliant and irresistible. Now I knew the balance of power among the peb had shifted.

My eyes flickered round the Gymna. Allyman dropped

from the ropes where he had been working, and stepped forward. He raised his right hand slightly. I saw the silvery covering on his forearm. I realised the peb were watching him constantly, as aware of him now as they had always been of Hythe, and for the same reasons. He had power over them and they were afraid of him. Then, like his mirror image, my brother stepped forward. He was wearing the silvery bandage too.

Into the tense silence, Leeward spoke directly to me. 'Ya talk ta dem!' he said. 'Ya talk ta de Vexa! Gal, I sab ya ken do dat. I sab ya be de wan.'

'Listen to me,' I said rapidly. 'There's very little time. Leeward, we're not in Space. Vexak is not a real planet. It's all a huge trick. We're still on Earth.'

He stared at me fixedly and then the light in his eyes changed, as though the animal had come in sight of safety. He put out his hand and very gently rested it on the side of my face. I put my hand up to his and clung on to it.

'Where's Hythe!' I said. 'We've got keys. We can get out, but we must go before Hythe gets here.' I glanced towards the doors, which had closed behind us, expecting at any moment to see them slide open again.

Leeward stared at me as the truth sank in. He believed me almost immediately, not because I gave him any proof – I didn't have time – but because it was me telling him. But when he finally spoke, his voice was slow and doubtful.

'Tings done change heah! Peter an Allyman in charge na.'

My eyes turned again to them. I could read it in the way they stood. Neither one of them had been able to challenge Leeward alone, but together they could. So even though they'd hated each other, they'd formed an alliance against him, encouraged of course, by Hythe. They were his henchmen now, second in command only to him.

I expected them to move, or speak, but they simply continued to watch me. Then Liane came up to me and touched me on the arm, checking I was real. 'Joey,' she said wonderingly. I thought she might hug me, but she didn't. She backed away from me to the wall where Bro Rabbit was sitting on his pole. She picked him up and put him on her hand.

'Waal, kiss ma ass,' Bro Rabbit growled mockingly. 'Wat place deez chilluns com fram?'

The peb had dropped noiselessly from the ropes and the trapezes, had uncoiled themselves from the wall bars and the floor, and were now gathered round us in a circle. Bro Rabbit's words made them look at him, releasing them a little from the power Allyman and Peter held over them.

'Ya gotta believe we,' Mariam said, holding out her hands to them. 'We is on Earss!'

They regarded us with suspicious eyes. One or two turned away sneering in disbelief.

'It de trus!' I said pleadingly. I spun round looking at each of them in turn. Fenja and Eduardo were standing next to Liane as if they were waiting to hear what Bro Rabbit thought. Presh was next to Allyman, and as I looked into their eyes he put his hand up and rested it on the back of her neck under her thick black hair. She leaned towards him. Her gaze was full of contempt for me. She had always despised me. Why should she change now? Allyman's grey eyes were opaque and cold, but his watchfulness told me something. I looked across from him to Peter.

Everything about my brother seemed more intense, as if the months in the Galax-Arena had brought out all his essential qualities and buffed away everything else. He looked incredibly fit, supercharged with energy and power. Like Allyman, he was watching me carefully, as if he was assessing how much I knew.

'You've got to believe me,' I said without much conviction. 'Peter, we've got a chance to escape!'

'Joey,' he replied gently. 'Joey, baby!' He sounded so compassionate and kind, so unlike my brother, so like ... like Hythe! And in that moment, I realised I was telling him nothing he didn't already know. Hythe had co-opted him totally, him and Allyman.

I looked from one redhead to the other. Allyman was fined down too, altered by grief and anger into a lean, silvery version of his old self. Yet, like Peter, the changes had not weakened him. They had made him stronger and much more powerful. With the two of them ranged against us, what hope did we have of getting away?

Peter raised his arm slightly and stepped towards me. I retreated, pulling Leeward back with me. 'Don't touch me,' I said. 'Keep away from me.'

He smiled kindly at me.

'Don't worry, Joey. Everything's gonna be just fine.'

I turned to the peb, stumbling over the words, trying to reach them and convince them before Peter silenced me. 'The Vexa aren't aliens,' I shouted. 'They're humans. One of them was my owner. She took off her mask and she was just an old woman in a costume. This place is being run by humans. You're not lost in Space. You don't have to despair. You're still on Earth!'

My heart was beating so fast I thought I was going to be sick. If Peter and Allyman didn't deal with me, at any moment Hythe would come through the doors and my life would be over. My words sounded like idiocy even to me. Again, I wondered if I had simply gone mad.

The peb obviously thought I had. But they weren't sure. They looked at each other, uneasy and alarmed.

'Ya mean we ken go home?' someone said.

'We ken go bak ta Earss?'

'We be on Earss,' Mariam said. 'We never leave it.'

For a moment I thought they were going to believe her. A movement, close to joy, started to run through them. But Allyman stepped forward, hand raised. The peb turned to him.

He was smiling, very slightly. Like Peter he knew I was telling the truth. He had been told. Hythe had told both of them before enrolling them in Project Genesis Five.

'We came in the space rocket,' Allyman said. 'That trip was real. We all went through it. We're performers in the Galax-Arena. That can't all be lies.' He looked around at the peb, and smiled more broadly at them. They relaxed a little. They had been told what to believe by their new trainer. They were willing to follow him.

'It be,' Mariam said. 'It be all lies. Fram start ta finis all lies. But na we is done wid de lyin. We is gon escape fram heah.'

'Ya be crazy lak yo sister, kid!' Presh taunted her. She put out a hand and flicked her scornfully on the shoulder. Mariam's face tightened. She stepped closer to Leeward and me.

'There's no such thing as space rockets,' I said. 'You can't travel at the speed of light. It's just not possible. We cannot be on a planet called Vexak light years away from Earth. There's no way we could get there.'

'But we done get dere,' Presh sneered. 'Dat ware we be!' I could tell she believed what she said. So Allyman had told no one else, not even her.

'People travel through space,' he said now, persuasively. 'We seen it on television.'

The peb nodded in assent. Of course people could travel through space – it was the basic stuff of all their fantasies and stories.

I looked at Mariam in despair. She shrugged her shoulders.

'Ony wan ting ta do,' she said. 'We bettah leave and leave na!'

'I'm not leaving without Peter and Liane,' I said stubbornly.

'It no use,' Leeward said. 'He wan of dem na!'

'No!' I shouted. 'No! Not Peter! You are not one of them, Peter. You are one of us! And you're coming with us. We're getting out of here!'

He looked at me with his bright eyes. He pulled at the covering on his arm as if it was bothering him. Then he looked at Allyman. Some message passed between them.

'No one's leaving,' Allyman said, cold. 'You're all staying here.'

'Allan,' Leeward said. 'Ya ken be wid we; ya ken com ta. Ya don gotta do wat dey tell ya. Ya ken fight it.'

Allyman shook his head. 'Don't believe them,' he said

to the peb. 'They've all gone mad. You step outside and you're gonna die. Hythe'll never even let you step outside, come to that. And who wants to go back anyway?' His chill voice rose above the bewildered murmuring of the peb, silencing them. 'What homes are you going back to, you dumb kids? You haven't got homes. You haven't got parents. You're the garbage of the world, you know that. No one needs you back there, no one wants you. You're disposable. You're waste. Good for nothing. But here you can be stars. Here you can be the champions. Don't chuck it all away!'

The peb looked at one another doubtfully.

'Don listen ta he,' Leeward shouted. 'We mak our own home. We be each udders familia.'

'Bullshit!' Allyman said. 'The only familia you're ever gonna have is right here.' His voice went soft and persuasive as he gazed round at them. 'You all know me,' he went on. 'You can trust me. Don't listen to this crazy loser who Hythe's given up on, and this fat, stupid kid who's never been a performer. What do they know about anything?'

The peb wavered. One or two let out their frustration and doubt in a quick succession of cartwheels across the floor. Eduardo dropped onto his hands. Upside down, he said, 'Wat Bro Rabbit say?'

Bro Rabbit waggled his ears and said nothing.

'Liane,' I said. 'You believe me, don't you? Don't you remember what Hayden used to say? "Blinding them with fake science." That's what Hythe's been doing. He's been blinding you with fake science. The whole thing is fake. You've got to believe me. I've never lied to you. Make Bro Rabbit tell them!'

Her eyes evaded mine. 'I don't make him,' she said slowly. 'He just says things.'

The moment was passing. We were losing most of the peb. It was too hard for them to change their view of the world so quickly. And what Allyman had said had got through to them. They had no future on Earth, back in the corrupt and cruel societies they had been stolen from.

They would never go home. Home had ceased to exist for them long before Hythe had appeared to kidnap – or rescue – them.

'Come on, Joey,' Peter said. His eyes held some warning for me behind his apparent concern. 'Give it up.'

'We've got to deal with her,' Allyman said.

'For God's sake,' Peter replied. 'She's my sister.'

'You're in the Galax-Arena, man. No brothers, no sisters, no friends. We've got to get rid of her!'

Peter came closer to me, took my arm, whispered in my ear, 'Give it away and I might be able to save you. Just pretend to give in. I'll fix it, I promise you.'

'Pretend?' I said. 'Pretend what? Pretend false is true and true false? I'm not doing that! If you're in charge here now, we can walk out! You can get us out.'

'It's too late for that,' Peter replied, fingering the silver covering with tense fingers.

'Ken ya fight dat ting?' Leeward questioned him.

Peter's eyes were distant as if he was listening, 'Effan ya wan, ya ken fight, sure. But who wan ta?'

I wrenched my arm away from him. I still held the card keys in my other hand. 'We're going,' I said to Liane. 'Come now.'

'I'm not going unless Fenja goes,' she said.

'Fenja!' I turned to her. Her face was impassive as always. She looked sideways at Presh. Presh made a scornful gesture with her hand and turned her back.

So only three of us, Leeward, Mariam and myself, moved towards the doors.

'Joey,' Peter said one last time.

'You're not going anywhere, kids,' Allyman sneered, raising his hand.

As the buzzing started, the doors gave a slight tremor.

I heard Leeward's voice through the sickness and terror inside my head. 'We ta late. Hyd com.'

15

Hythe, usually so controlled and cool, was in a state of fury. I had thought I wanted to confront him, but now that he was here I was terrified. My first instinct was to grab Leeward's hand. My next was to hide – but there was nowhere to hide. I just managed to slip the keys down the front of my leotard.

The peb felt his rage. Some of them simply sank down to the ground, cowering. Others took up their routines frantically as though they could escape his anger by showing him they were working hard.

But when he spoke his voice was light. 'This is off bounds for you and Joella now,' he said to Mariam. 'Come on, I'll take you back.' Then he turned to me, 'Say goodbye, Joey, babes.'

I knew he meant it. Goodbye to everything, goodbye for ever. He wasn't going to take us back. He was going to kill us.

'Don touch dem,' Leeward shouted. 'Keep bak! We sab de trus na. Ya gotta lat we go!'

'Lat ya go!' Hythe repeated mocking him. 'Ya ken go! You're free to walk out of here. You all know that. Only problem is, kiddo, you'd crumple up in a millisecond. You're on Vexak, didja forget that?'

'We know we're not,' I said. 'We know all about it – all

about the experiments, everything. Emmeline told us.'

'Ware be dat ol woman?' Mariam put in.

'There is no old woman,' Hythe said dismissing her with a wave. 'You must have been hallucinating. Often happens. Now move it. No more chit chat. Let's go!'

He made a twirling movement with his hand up towards his forehead. Some of the peb laughed.

'She's raving,' Allyman said. 'They're both crazy mad.' He and Peter had moved slightly closer together, and were facing the peb, like armed guards.

I wondered briefly what had happened to Emmeline. Either dead by now, or silenced in some other way with drugs or threats or both. Hythe wanted us out of the way as quickly as possible before we unsettled the rest of the peb, but the thought of her made me determined not to go quietly.

'You lied to us,' I yelled as loudly as I could. 'You lied to us about everything. He stole you,' I told the peb. 'He done teef ya, an he gon kill ya. Wan ya ta ol ta perform, ya all gon die.'

Something echoed like an enormously loud whisper through the Gyma. *Hip, hop hai, ya all gon die.* The peb's attention turned to Bro Rabbit who was still sitting on Liane's hand. Eduardo began to jump from foot to foot, chanting under his breath.

'Shut up!' Hythe must have felt his control slipping then for he lifted his hand and the menacing buzzing started in my head. I felt it reach through my brain. I saw the girl being punished, but I didn't hate her. I felt sorry for her. I knew she was right. I wanted her to speak again. She did. She said haltingly, 'We . . . are . . . still . . . on . . . Earth.'

Hythe grabbed me by the shoulder. 'Move it,' he ordered. 'Mariam, Leeward, you too. Out of here.' When the three of us struggled and resisted he shouted, 'Move it, I said!'

Bro Rabbit said, 'Ya move it, apeface! Ya be de wan gon die.'

One of the peb laughed nervously, a short mirth-less cackle.

'Quit your games, sweetheart,' Hythe said to Liane. 'It was cute once, but now it's boring.'

Bro Rabbit waggled his ears. His bright blue eyes shone. He growled evilly. 'Ya be wan wicked man. Na be de tyam fo ya ta pay!'

'For God's sake, let's get rid of this kidding toy once and for all,' Hythe muttered. He made a snatch at the rabbit, but his hand seemed to go wide of it.

'Woo!' Bro Rabbit said and shook his ears. He growled warningly, 'Ya be makin wan big mistake, apeface!'

There was another short laugh. I saw Hythe's muscles go tense.

'Peter,' he said. 'You deal with it.'

'Put Bro down, Liane,' Peter said. 'It's making Hythe angry.'

'Ya watch yo mouth,' Bro said. 'Don ya spik ta yo sister lak dat!'

'Liane,' Peter pleaded, 'Give Bro to me!'

Once again Bro seemed to shift rapidly out of reach. 'Woo!' He shook his ears again. 'Cyan ketch me!' he crowed.

'Use your hand on her,' Hythe ordered.

Peter went pale.

'Use it!'

Peter raised his bandaged hand slowly, then lowered it. 'I can't,' he said. 'I can't use it on her. She's my sister.'

'Last chance,' Hythe said.

'Peter,' I yelled, 'Don't do it.'

'Allyman!' Hythe said. Allyman raised his hand, a smile on his thin lips. The buzzing started. Bro Rabbit screamed.

He screamed louder than the buzzing. He screamed with pain and outrage for all the peb. All their loneliness and terror was in that scream, and all their anger and hate. Liane's mouth was wide open, and her eyes were closed. The sound came from the depths of her being as if only her death would stop it.

'Leave her alone!' Peter yelled and threw himself at Allyman. Hythe stepped forward to intervene. He had his back to us. Leeward gave a rapid sign to me and Mariam, and we jumped him from behind.

His strength was enormous. We could barely hold him down between us. Mariam covered his arm with her thin, strong body, wrapping herself round it so he could not lift it to use it on us. But even though I had wanted to destroy him, and rage and hatred were clouding my brain like red fog, I could feel myself faltering. I know he never stopped talking, as though he could still reach us and dominate us, and I remember thinking that his voice could never be silenced. He was too powerful for us to kill him.

The screaming stopped with a sudden indrawn breath. As Allyman and Peter struggled on the floor, and as Hythe threshed and rolled beneath the three of us, Bro Rabbit spoke again.

'Go!' he said, 'Go, go, go! Kill him. Kill de wicked man. All ya chilluns dat he treat sho bad. Na is de tyam!'

Eduardo leapt forward. He held his little knife in his hand. I saw it gleam as he stabbed at Hythe again and again. Presh had her hands round my throat, and my sight went dark. I heard in a daze Hythe's voice, Bro Rabbit's growling, and then a terrible sound from the peb as their control broke completely.

He had always treated them like animals, and now they responded like animals. Their trainer was helpless on the ground and they turned on him and tore him to pieces.

16

Heydoo, horrodoo, makashaka, haidoo.
Marradoo, corradoo, hakkarakka, maidoo.
Eduardo danced and chanted, wild with excitement and
terror, the knife held high above his head, as one by one
the peb drew back from Hythe's mutilated body.

There was blood everywhere. We were all painted with
it as though for some travesty performance.

The peb looked around at each other with dulling eyes.
Never before had they seemed so truly and utterly lost.
Most of them still believed they were exiled millions of
miles from Earth. Now they had destroyed the one thing
that had been constant in their lives. Many were sobbing,
tears and blood mingling on their thin cheeks.

Leeward was ashen with shock, staring at the blood on
his hands. I looked at my own. They were just as bloody. I
tried to wipe them on my legs. I could feel shock coming
on me too, paralysing my body and brain. I didn't know
what to do next. I wanted someone to tell me what to do. I
looked at Peter. He was as pale as death, a splash of
darkening blood on his forehead, almost the same colour
as his hair.

He did not look back at me. He was staring at Allyman.
Then he looked down to the ground as, moving like

robots, they both stepped towards Hythe's body. They knelt beside it, touched what was left of the arm covering. For a few moments they were as lost and uncertain as the rest of the peb, but they were listening.

All my instincts were shrieking at me, 'Run! Get out of here while there's still a fraction of a chance.' I turned towards the doors. Something was digging into my ribs. I put my hand down the front of my leotard. Of course, it was Emmeline's card keys. My brain was working very slowly, one thought at a time. *She had left them for us in the elevator so we could get out.* Mariam was still on the floor. I reached out and touched her on the shoulder. Showing her the keys I said, 'We can get out of here.'

She rose slowly to her feet. I held my hands out to the peb, so they could see the keys too. 'We can get out of here,' I repeated. They looked back at me with their lost, unreachable eyes. Only Liane moved towards me, followed by her shadows, Fenja and Eduardo.

'You all stay here,' Allyman ordered, leaping to his feet. 'Everything's going on just the same. Don't move!' And he raised his hand, the silvery covering splashed with blood.

The peb sighed, and relaxed a little. Allyman had taken over. He was going to tell them what to do.

'Stay heah, die heah!' The growling voice of Bro Rabbit interrupted him. Bro Rabbit was covered in blood and he looked like some horrible fetish. 'Run na, chilluns, whyal ya has de tyam.'

Then Liane said in her own voice, sounding just like she did at home when she wanted Peter and me to play with her, 'Come on, Peter, come on, Joey! Let's go!'

'But we no gonna jus walk outta dis place!' Mariam said. 'Dey no gon let we walk out!' Her voice was quavering.

'I don't care,' I said stubbornly. 'Emmeline gave us the keys so we could get out. And I'm going.'

'Dey kill we!' Mariam said.

'Dey kill we heah," Leeward said.

Liane was already at the doors.

'Come on, Joey!' she said. 'Bro says to hurry. Open the doors!'

I walked over to them and opened them. Mariam and Leeward came with me. Eduardo and Fenja followed Liane. No one else. They watched us go.

'We can't go without Peter,' I said to Liane.

I turned one last time and called out to him. But he was gazing intently at Allyman as though they were both listening to something.

'Hurry,' Liane said, and pulled at Fenja. Fenja was also making one last appeal, calling out before the doors closed. 'Presh, Presh, run na, ya ken com ta!'

But Presh did not move away from Allyman.

Outside in the corridor it was totally silent. I had no hope of escape, really. I never believed they would let us walk away from Project Genesis Five. I thought they were playing some horrible cat-and-mouse game with us. Whatever we did would be some form of experiment to them. Right now someone was watching us, recording every move we made as if we were rats in a maze. And like laboratory rats it didn't matter if we were smart or dumb – we would die in the end. But I didn't know what else to do. None of us did. Once again, the only way seemed to be forward. So we stumbled down the corridor to the elevator.

I was just thinking about how Liane and Peter had gambolled down the corridor like dogs, when I heard the pad of feet behind us. Peter came round the curve, his colour restored a little, his eyes bright.

'Hey, wait,' he said, 'I'm coming with you.'

'Dey lat ya go?' Leeward said, indicating his bandaged arm.

'Oh, this is nothing,' Peter replied, breathing fast. 'They can't keep me here if I don't want to stay. And look, I've got . . .' he stumbled as he tried to say the name . . . 'Hythe's keys.'

He held up a set of card keys, along with something else: a key ring with a little silver shark hanging from it. Car keys – not for a spaceship, not for the Skyshark, just for the Landcruiser that had met us at the station.

'Come on, kiddo,' Peter said to me, as the elevator doors

opened in response to the card. 'We're getting out of here. Trust me!'

Fenja was the first in, grabbing Eduardo by the hand, and pulling him after her. The rest of us followed, Peter last. We looked in bemusement at the buttons, with their numbers and strange symbols. We had no idea which one to press. We had never been above the floor we were on now, labelled G for Gymna and Galax-Arena.

'Which button?' I said to Peter, but he was already pressing the highest, number 21.

'Ground floor,' he said. 'We're going out!'

'Twenty-one is the ground? Peter, have we been underground all this time?'

'It is the most amazing complex,' he said, his voice quiet and awed. 'It's unbelievable.'

'How much do you know? How much have they told you?'

The elevator shuddered very slightly as it rose upward. Peter shrugged. 'I can't tell you anything, really. It's all top secret. But it's wonderful. They're making the most incredible advances. We should be proud to have been part of it.'

'Wat ya sayin?' Mariam snapped at him. 'We be proud of all dat teefin an killin an dess?' She drew away from him, and leant against the side of the lift. Beads of sweat were standing out on her forehead. She wiped them away with her hand.

'Ya truly takin we out?' Leeward demanded. 'Or is ya handin we over ta dem?'

'Don't worry so much, Leeward, baby,' Peter said. 'It's all cool, hey, man?'

We were all, except for him, huddled now in one corner of the elevator. He surveyed us with an indulgent grin. 'Don't worry,' he said again. 'You can trust your old uncle, can't cha?'

The elevator sped upward. The acceleration of the lift reminded me of something I remembered from a nightmare. My stomach lurched. Eduardo clapped his hands to his mouth. Fenja rolled her eyes upwards, a greenish tinge on her brown skin.

'Sho far, sho good,' Bro Rabbit growled suddenly and the elevator stopped.

I looked at the others. They were all pale, not only from the speed of the ascent but also from terror. I was sure we were trapped. The doors would open and we would be caught. *They* would be waiting there like the cat outside the mouse hole, the scientists at the end of the maze.

The doors opened. There was no one there.

It hadn't been dark in the passages or the elevator. They had all been lit by the same artificial light as within the Galax-Arena. Outside the elevator the hexagonal entrance hall was also brightly lit, but beyond it was blackness. We blinked at it, not sure for a moment what it was.

When Mariam and I had run from the tank to the Gymna, we had thought it was morning, *manyan*. In that artificial deceitful man-made world it *was* morning, but outside, on planet Earth, it was night.

We hesitated on the threshold of the lift.

'We is walkin inta dere trap!' Leeward said.

'Everything's fine,' Peter said, and led us out. We followed him to the main doors. He opened them swiftly and competently, getting the right key first time. I had a moment of piercing terror that I had been wrong after all and that we would be stepping out into that alien atmosphere that Hythe had so often warned us about, but when the doors swung open the air did not choke us, nor did the atmosphere crush us. Gravity held us as firmly as it had in the Galax-Arena and in our former lives. We ran out into the night.

Away from the bright lights, I could see the stars above our heads. The air was sharp and very cold. Winter air. I made out Orion and Vela. I wondered where the Cygni system was and if I could see it from here. Then I looked behind me and saw the domed buildings. I saw the jets on the tarmac, and the glint of the fake rocket. Parked among other ordinary everyday trucks, I saw the Landcruiser.

We had never left the air base. We had been there all the time.

I looked up at the stars where we had believed ourselves to be. I felt as if the Galax-Arena spun and shimmered above me and then burst into a million tiny particles to be dispersed in the universe. It had existed only in our minds.

We all stayed close to Peter. He was the only one who seemed to know what he was doing. He exuded all his old confidence together with a newer quality of leadership. He acted as if he expected us to follow him, and we did.

Eduardo exclaimed, 'Dat de plane I flied on!' and Leeward muttered that he recognised it too.

'Sho ware in hell we be?' Mariam said in my ear as we followed Peter across the dark grounds towards the vehicles.

'This is where Hythe brought us,' I said. 'It's somewhere in Australia.'

'Australia?' Mariam said in disbelief.

'It might be quite close to my aunt's place,' I went on. 'But I don't know how close. We drove a long way . . .'

My voice trailed away. Talking about Aunt Jill had suddenly brought her close to me. I might see her again after all.

Ahead of us Peter was opening the door of the Landcruiser.

'What are you doing?' I hissed at him.

'Hop in' he said, getting in himself. 'All of you, hop in. We're taking the Tojo.' He held the keys up to me with a grin, threw them in the air and caught them, and then slipped them into the ignition.

The engine started up with a roar as we all piled in. I looked around, but no one came running.

'They're not just letting us go!' I said.

'Course they are,' Peter replied with a laugh. 'We're the good guys. The good guys always get away!'

He reversed the big car neatly out of the parking space and gunned it towards the gates.

'Better get down,' he said. 'This is where we might have some trouble. I'm going through fast so hang on.'

The younger ones slid off their seats onto the floor and we huddled down over them. There were lights on in the guard house and at any moment I expected us to be challenged. But the Landcruiser hardly slowed as we went through.

It bucked and swayed and, as I was thrown sideways, I looked up at Peter. I was really impressed at how well he was handling the car – after all it was months since we had driven with Hayden. I saw him give a thumbs up to the dark shapes behind the windows.

17

'Not a problem,' Peter said, putting a hand out to ruffle Eduardo's hair. The others let out a cheer, and came jumping up onto the seats like puppies. We had all been in the back, but now the younger three pushed forward onto the front seat. Eduardo couldn't stop caressing the controls of the car, his fingers running over the gearstick, and the dashboard. Liane and Fenja had their arms round each other and were touching noses – they looked years younger as though they had suddenly rediscovered their childhood. Mariam held my arm tightly while tears rolled silently down her face.

'Ya did it, man,' Leeward said, ecstatic. 'Ya did it. We is free!' He looked back over his shoulder. I followed his look. For a moment we saw the lights of the air base, then the car skidded round a corner and there was nothing behind us but the dark bush, lit only by the red tail lights.

'Open de window,' Leeward told me. 'I gotta breathe dat air!'

Peter had to press a central switch. The night air came in, real and freezing. We were all barefoot, still in leotards. I was shivering with cold and excitement, and something else. I wanted to forget the thumbs up but I couldn't.

'Peter,' I said, leaning forward and speaking into his ear. 'Where are we going?'

'It's all under control,' he said cheerfully. 'I know exactly what I'm doing!'

'Do you have any idea where we are?'

'Yup!'

'Well, are we anywhere near Aunt Jill's! Is that where we're going?'

'Good old Aunt Jill!' Peter exclaimed, and put his foot down as the road straightened. 'It's a long way,' he went on. 'You guys had better get some zeez. Liane, get the chocolate out of the glove box and give everyone a bit. Then you can put your heads down and leave everything to me.'

'Peter,' I said, 'What the hell is going on?'

He began to whistle *Maria* softly.

'Answer me, God damn it!' I shook him on the shoulder. He took his right hand from the wheel and held it up to me.

'Just cool it, Joey,' he said. 'Cool it. Don't ask any questions. Just do as I say. We'll get away, but you've got to do as I say. Eat your chocolate and go to sleep.'

I took the piece Liane handed to me. It looked like ordinary chocolate. I thought of the fake space food we'd been eating for months, and I remembered the coffee and the chocolate biscuits we'd eaten in this very car. Nobody was going to deceive me like that again. I was just about to lean past Leeward and drop the chocolate out of the open window, when there was a click as Peter forestalled me. The windows rose and the doors locked.

'Better keep them locked now,' Peter said. 'I don't want anyone falling out. I'm going to drive to where we can find someone to help us. But that place was pretty isolated. It'll take a while.' I dropped my chocolate on the floor. I wanted to tell the others not to eat it, but I didn't want Peter to hear me, and anyway they gobbled it up too quickly.

I nearly asked for another bit so I could gobble some too. Just the smell made my mouth water. I was starving. I had to hold my mouth shut with my hands, so I wouldn't give in.

Peter drove steadily and carefully down a dirt road that

seemed to go on forever. It reminded me of some of the tracks we had explored with Hayden. We used to drive all day without meeting another vehicle. A couple of times we'd had a flat tyre, and while we'd been fixing it by the side of the road not one car had passed us. It scared me sometimes, wondering what would happen if we met with a real emergency. It could be days before anyone found us.

I had the same feeling now. Beyond the lights of the Landcruiser, lay the bush, immense and dark. There were no other lights around, no houses, no cars, nothing. I felt like a time traveller in a tiny capsule, hurtling towards another reality that I wasn't sure I could cope with. I couldn't imagine what it was going to be like back in the world we had once called the real one. What would people think when we suddenly turned up again, having been lost for months? And what would they make of our companions? Would anyone believe our story?

I thought of my parents and Aunt Jill. Would they take us back? Of course they would, I told myself. But Aunt Jill didn't like children and was suspicious of foreigners. And Hayden and Sylvie hadn't been able to make a home for three children. What would they do with four more, who were not even really children? My hands against my face smelled of blood. We had killed a man. Would we be sent to prison? More likely a loony bin.

I was afraid. Too much had happened for us simply to go home. Hythe had been right. You can't go home. Once you've been made to grow up, you can never go home again. When we had been captured we had been children: innocents. But since then we had lived in the Galax-Arena among the peb. We were the peb. None of us was innocent now.

Perhaps the others were thinking the same thoughts. Or perhaps, as I suspected, the chocolate was laced with a tranquilliser. Anyway, the exuberance and chattering ceased as one by one they fell silent. Fenja slept with her mouth open, snoring a little. Eduardo muttered something in a dream. Next to me I felt Mariam relax. Her grip on my arm slackened and her breathing evened. Even

Leeward, on the other side, was dozing, his head rolling forward on his chest.

I wished I could see into their heads and share their dreams. But then it occurred to me that they were more likely to be nightmares, the nightmares of the exiled and homeless all over the Earth. Perhaps Allyman had been right; perhaps they should never have left the Galax-Arena. I should have stayed in the tank. I should never have dragged them away. I should have kept quiet. I should never have seen the truth, let alone told anyone else about it.

Peter spoke suddenly. 'Are you awake, Joey?'

In the rear-view mirror I saw his eyes seek mine. 'You didn't eat the chocolate,' he said, 'I didn't think you would. Joey, Joey, what are we going to do with you?'

'You tell me,' I said. 'You're the one that seems to know what's going on. So you tell me what's happening and what's going to happen.'

His eyes had returned to the road and he was silent for a few minutes. When he spoke again, I could hardly hear him. He seemed to be speaking to himself as much as to me.

'I thought we were on Vexak,' he said, 'I thought we were exiled for ever. So when Hythe asked me, I said I'd join them. What else could I do? What other options were there? Allan had already agreed. I wasn't going to let him get ahead of me. I'd just got to the top. I had to stay there. I could see what was happening to Leeward. He was on the way out. I didn't want to go that way. I wanted to survive.'

'Didn't you know about the whole set-up?' I said. 'What about Project Genesis Five?'

'The old woman told you that, did she? I didn't know about it until after they'd fixed my arm. I truly thought they were Vexa – aliens. How did you find out?'

'There was a fly in the tank we were kept in,' I said. 'I figured it out.'

'Witch,' he said.

'What will happen to Emmeline?'

'The old woman? They'll probably help her to die. She

broke the rules by talking to you so she can't carry on with the programme and, even though in theory the clients are free to leave, no one ever gets out alive. They're written off as failed experiments. There are plenty of others to take their place. The waiting list goes on for ever.'

I thought, poor Emmeline, who was afraid of dying and who would never get outside now. Then I thought, *no one gets out alive*. The peb were right: *out de dar an inta dess*. It was going to be the same for us.

'What are you going to do with us?' I said to Peter. 'Are you taking us somewhere to kill us?'

'You really are a witch, Joey,' he replied, shaking his head. 'You really do have second sight.'

'No,' I said. 'I just use my eyes. And then I tell people what I see. Anyone could do it.'

'I'm hoping they won't kill you,' he said slowly, as if he was listening to something. 'I think they might spare you and Liane. Of course you'll have to work with them, but they think you've both got enormous potential.'

'So they'll spare us?' I repeated. 'That's very generous of them! If it's not just one more lie. How can you believe anything that comes out of that place?'

'I'm trying to save you,' he said. He was sounding angry now too. 'It's not easy. They want you out of the way. They think you'd be better dead.'

'That's why I don't believe in their kind offer. Anyway, I'd never work with them. I'd rather be dead.'

'You hate me for joining them, don't you?'

I felt an enormous hopelessness. For a long time I said nothing. Then Peter said, 'I didn't have any other choice.'

'Fine,' I said. 'None of us had any choice. We can only do what's in our nature to do. You take your path, I'll take mine. But one of us is going to have to die at the end of it.'

'I wish we had left you behind at the station,' he burst out. 'You were never meant to come. If Hythe hadn't brought you he would still be alive.'

'Hythe killed people!' I replied, furious. 'He kidnapped and stole children and made them die in terrible ways. And you were going to do the same. You were going to be like him.'

'He was cool,' Peter said sadly. 'I loved him.'

After that neither of us spoke. The car raced on through the night.

My thoughts went round and round but I was calm inside, as though I was observing them from a great distance. I stared through the window at the bush outside, remembering how I had seen it flying past from the train on the way to Casino. I wished I could be out in it. Our one brief moment in the real world had made me long for more. I wanted to feel the air on my face and the earth under my feet. I wanted desperately to be somewhere that wasn't man-made. I thought I might be going to die, but I didn't really care, as long as I felt the air on my face first.

Peter drove on, tireless as a robot. I wondered how much the thing in his arm controlled him, as well as allowing him to control others. I wondered if Hythe had been controlled in the same way. We had killed him – but two more had arisen to take his place, like the dragon's heads.

I thought, I could reach past Peter, seize the wheel of the Landcruiser, and send it spinning off the road. We would all overpower him and escape – but the others still slept their drugged sleep, the doors were locked, and I was afraid if I did crash the car it would burst into flames. Even if it didn't, and we all got out alive, what would we do with Peter? As long as he was under *their* control he could control us. I remembered the buzzing from Hythe's hand and how it had penetrated to the centre of my being. I recalled hearing myself say the words 'We are still on Earth,' and I felt sick from shock. I thought about the girl from Chicago who had defied him until she went mad. All her defiance did no good in the end. She still died.

Then I thought the unthinkable – would Peter have to die so we could escape?

Peter could not die. He was indestructible, the immortal, golden one. So I did the only thing left to me. Nothing.

18

My throat was dry and my eyes sticky. My head ached. Slowly the world outside became grey. The headlights paled. I could see now where we were – on an endless dirt road that wound upwards along the side of a narrow gully. It was no more than a vehicle's width, and on the low side the drop was almost sheer.

Peter shifted down as the climb steepened, but as he let the clutch out the engine stalled. The Landcruiser rolled slightly backwards. I grabbed onto the back of the seat. I could see the accident coming: we were going to go off the edge, out of control, but Peter pulled on the handbrake and got the car started again. He must have been a bit unnerved himself, for we set off with a series of jolts and jerks that shook the others out of their sleep.

They rubbed their eyes, tried to stretch, complained of being thirsty and needing to pee. They all looked terrible, faces streaked with tears and blood, eyes dark from drugs and fear. Peter cheered them up, joked with them and promised we would make a stop really soon. By the time everyone was fully awake, the slope had lessened. We came over the crest, and halted on the edge of the escarpment.

The road ran along the top of the ridge. Behind us lay the thickly wooded gullies we had come through; in front a grassy slope led to the edge. Peter unlocked the car and we climbed stiffly out.

A few straggly trees clung to the brink of the escarpment and we could see the tops of others that grew precariously out of the cliff. Otherwise there was no vegetation until the valley floor below where I could make out a dense rainforest tangle of ferns and palms. Beyond the rainforest, coastal plains stretched away towards a golden shimmer that had to be the ocean. The sun was about to rise.

I stared at it all in wonder, feasting my eyes on it. I think we all did. After the starkness of our surroundings in captivity it looked so rich and alive. Birds were shrieking from the valley. I was astonished at how loud and unafraid they sounded.

The sun's warmth brought out insects. Flies were starting to settle on us and I could hear mosquitoes whine in my ear. I didn't slap at them. I thought I would never kill an insect again.

Then I remembered that we had killed a man and I started to shiver. I looked at Peter. He was leaning against the side of the Landcruiser. He glowed all over in the early morning light. The bandage on his arm had gone pinkish in the sun.

Now what, I thought.

As if in response he grinned at me. 'Pretty good, hey,' he said. 'Didn't I tell you the good guys always get away? And you're not only the good guys, you lot. You're the champs. The greatest!' He looked round at us all, smiling cheerfully, irresistibly. 'So now we're going to put on a show. The last and the best. Leeward, baby, you reckon you're a great acrobat, doncha?'

Leeward, standing at my side, gazing like me in wonder at the newfound world, shook his head.

'Who sab?' he muttered. 'Dat all finis na. I bin new born. Who sab wat I be?'

'I got news for you, man,' Peter said, raising his arm slightly. 'It's not finished. Not quite. This is your last performance, guys. Better make it the best.'

They were all staring at him now: Liane and Fenja close together with Bro Rabbit sitting on Liane's hand between them, Eduardo just behind them, Mariam, Leeward and I a little closer to the edge.

'It's a competition,' Peter said. 'Let's see who the real stars are! Who can do the best leap with the most somersaults! I'll give you points. So who's going first? Fenja? Eduardo?'

No one answered him. No one moved.

The buzzing started very faintly.

'Looks like it'll have to be you, Leeward, mate. That's fitting. The boss should go first.'

'Ya gon mak we all kill oursel?' Leeward spoke quite calmly.

'I'm not making anyone kill themselves! That's entirely up to you. I'm just getting things rolling.'

'Wat bout yo sisters? Ya gon kill dem ta?'

'You'll never know that. Now jump!' The buzzing was loud now, making us all move towards the edge.

Leeward flinched. 'Don do dat,' he said. 'I gon jump, but freely, no cos ya is forcin me.'

'You really think it makes a difference,' Peter sneered.

Through the pain in my head I felt Leeward's hand touch the side of my face for one last time. I knew he was going to die. I grabbed at him, felt his strong, muscled catcher's arm, but then my grasp slipped and he took two swift steps that brought him to the edge.

I screamed as I saw him jump. Peter, facing us, smiled slightly but he did not try to stop me as I stepped closer to the edge. I looked down. My vision swam. Leeward had vanished completely. I thought the trees on the valley floor must have swallowed him up, but then I saw a movement among the leaves of one of the scrubby trees on the cliff face. He had leapt straight into it, grasped a branch and now, out of Peter's sight, was scrabbling to climb back up.

I looked back at Peter, trying to hide hope, trying to feign horror and despair. Not that I had to try all that hard. Even if Leeward succeeded in climbing back up, he

would be forced to jump again. We all would. I didn't
believe Peter when he said he would try and save Liane
and me. I was certain no one ever came alive out of
Project Genesis Five, unless they came out like Hythe,
like Peter, semi-robots controlled by the central power.

'Not very spectacular,' Peter said, '2.9, 3, maybe. Now
who's going next? Who can do better?'

Eduardo made a dash away, trying to get behind the
Landcruiser, trying vainly to find somewhere to hide.

'Hey, Ed, baby,' Peter said. 'Come back here, grommet!'

Eduardo came back, crawling on his stomach, his hands
clutching his head.

'You'd better go next,' Peter said kindly.

He's killing us like flies, I thought. I shouted to him.
'You can't do this to us, Peter. Don't do it. Don't be one of
them. We can get home now. Come back with us.' But
even as I said it, I knew I would never get through to him.
We were in his power and he was in *theirs*. If it had only
been him I might have reached him, but I was arguing
through him with all the power and wealth of the project.

He took no notice of me, but perhaps the sound of my
voice distracted him a little, for the buzzing seemed to
ease off and into the silence Bro Rabbit spoke. His
growly voice echoed round the escarpment, mocking,
challenging.

'Who dis kid tink he be? He tink he be de boss man?
Waal, de boss man dead. Don lat he live agen!'

'Hyd be dead,' Mariam said, stepping towards Peter. 'Ya
cyan mak we do nada. Ya be jus a kid!'

He raised his hand to her. The noise increased. My head
started to split with it. But Mariam still went forward.

'Jus a kid!' Bro Rabbit shouted. His voice was so loud it
seemed to reverberate up from the valley floor. 'He don
got no power ovah ya! He be jus a kid!' While I listened to
Bro I didn't hear the buzzing so badly. We all somehow
found the strength to close round Peter in a circle.

'Get back!' he shouted.

Mariam put her hand out and seized his arm. Peter
pushed her away. The buzzing was so loud now it was

more like a screaming. It made me retch and shake. But we staggered towards him, grasping at him and pulling him down.

We held him down while time stood still. Bro shouted and encouraged us and the buzzing grew stronger. I no longer knew who I was or what was happening. It took me to a place I knew I would never return from. But just as I thought I must die at any moment the noise stopped abruptly. It was replaced by something else, equally horrible but human. Peter was screaming.

We drew back from him. He was clutching his arm. The silver bandage was slashed away. Blood streamed from a deep wound. His hand dangled uselessly.

Eduardo stood on the edge of the cliff. His headband had fallen off. It lay at his feet, and his hair blew in the wind. He held up both hands triumphantly. In one he held his knife, in the other, the electronic gadget that had been implanted in Peter's arm. Proudly he showed them to us, chanting his menacing song, stamping in glee. Then he kissed the air in front of the device, kissed it goodbye and threw it over the edge.

Peter stopped screaming for a moment, looked at his arm, looked around at us. His eyes filled with tears. 'Joey,' he said, sounding like my brother again. 'Oh God, Joey, I've stuffed everything up.' He looked at his useless hand and began to sob.

I looked around desperately for something to staunch the blood. Peter shook his head, pushed the hair out of his eyes with his good hand, and went still. He seemed to be centering himself, as though he was preparing for a performance . . .

'No!' I shouted, trying to grab him as he took two quick, dancing steps to the edge.

He turned back to look at me. 'You did it, witch,' he said. 'You brought us home! Don't try to stop me. It's the best way out!'

He breathed deeply, raised his arms. The blood splashed down as he leaped upwards, the sun glinting on his hair.

It would have been a perfect way for him to go. The

heroic sacrifice at dawn. But it wasn't to be like that. It's harder to live than die. We were all frozen, watching the last, greatest performance but, as Peter leaped, Leeward came up over the edge of the cliff, bounding up as if he'd been catapulted, and caught him before he could fall.

For a few seconds they teetered, clasped together on the edge. Then we unfroze and rushed forwards to drag them both to safety. The flow of blood from Peter's wound lessened under Leeward's grip. I bent down and picked up Eduardo's headband. Mariam took it from me and bound it tightly round his wrist. No one said anything. Peter's colour had gone, as if he was fading away. When Leeward let go, he sank to the ground.

I looked around. I couldn't believe *they* weren't watching us still. The Landcruiser stood on the edge of the cliff, white and shiny, like an advertisement for a recreational vehicle. I hated it and everything it stood for. I ran to it, wrenched open the door, pulled off the handbrake, and leaped back as it began to roll. It rolled gently to the edge and dived bonnet first off the cliff.

As it hit the bottom and burst into flames, Bro Rabbit spoke for the last time, 'Na it be finis chilluns. Na ya ken all go home!'

And for a little while, we believed that we could . . .